Sticking her hands in the pockets of her jeans, Murphy turned to gaze at the view from the porch. A cool breeze lifted her hair, and she moved to sink down on the top step, out from under the porch roof, where the sun could warm her. Just sitting here on the Darlingtons' front porch dulled the picture of Rex's empty house in her head.

Leeda sat down beside her and leaned back on her palms, tapping her heels against the stairs. "It's really good to be here," she said.

Murphy looked at her quizzically. "Hey, how was the will reading?"

Leeda sighed, still staring out at the trees. "I inherited the ponies."

Murphy let out a guffaw. "The minis? The My Little Ponys?"

"And half a million dollars."

Murphy stopped mid-guffaw.

Peaches novels by

jodi lynn anderson

Peaches
THE Secrets OF Peaches
Love AND Peaches

Love and Peaches

a novel by

jodi lynn anderson

HARPER TEEN
An Imprint of HarperCollins Publishers

HarperTeen is an imprint of HarperCollins Publishers.

alloyentertainment
Produced by Alloy Entertainment
151 West 26th Street, New York, NY 10001

Library of Congress Cataloging-in-Publication Data
Anderson, Jodi Lynn.
    Love and peaches / Jodi Lynn Anderson. — 1st ed.
        p. cm.
    Summary: After their freshman year at different universities, Birdie, Leeda, and
Murphy return to Bridgewater, Georgia, for one last summer at the peach orchard where
they became best friends, and where they now face secrets, doubts, and new responsi-
bilities.
    ISBN 978-0-06-073313-1
    [1. Best friends—Fiction. 2. Friendship—Fiction. 3. Interpersonal relations—
Fiction. 4. Farm life—Georgia—Fiction. 5. Peach—Fiction. 6. Georgia—Fiction.]
I. Title.
PZ7.A53675Lov 2008   2008035522
[Fic]—dc22   CIP
                                                                                  AC

Typography by Andrea C. Uva
09 10 11 12 13   CG/RRDH   10 9 8 7 6 5 4 3 2 1
❖
First paperback edition, 2009

For Jan

Before

The Darlington Orchard in Bridgewater, Georgia, had seen its share of love affairs.

Some of them, like the blooming love between Poopie Pedraza and Walter Darlington and the roller-coaster romance between Murphy McGowen and Rex Taggart, had been out in the open, plain as day. Others had been secret, hidden under the shade of the trees, stolen in moments, never revealed.

But even these left traces.

A box of letters sat tucked in a closet on the upper floor of Primrose Cottage, waiting to spill its guts. An envelope arrived at #504 Anthill Acres Trailer Park, regarding the past of an eighteen-year-old girl. A ring dotted with tiny diamonds was removed from where it had been hidden for over fifty years and dropped into a Jiffy mailer.

Poopie Pedraza would have told you it was ghosts of these things being stirred up. She believed in all sorts of ghosts. Ghosts of the peaches that had grown there. Ghosts of dead pecan trees. Ghosts of long walks and swims in the lake. She told everyone who would listen that she believed in lost souls too, because once she had been one.

In the late spring, a nervous little Chihuahua was dropped off by the side of the road five miles outside Bridgewater and left to fend for itself. Judge Miller Abbott, the town justice, lost his wife and wondered how he would ever feel like his heart was whole again. A Mexican boy tucked a tiny box into his backpack and hoped.

Far away, in New York and Mexico City, Birdie, Leeda, and Murphy were blissfully oblivious to the fact that the ghosts were calling them home.

One

The grassy lawn of Columbia University was a vivid green, and Leeda Cawley-Smith lay entwined with her boyfriend, letting the sun's rays seep into her heavily SPFed skin. They were a T; she was perpendicular to him with her head on his stomach, big black sunglasses shielding her eyes. He had his knees up and a school catalog of summer classes covering his face. Occasionally someone appeared and hovered over them to say hello, as if they were Jackie and John F. Kennedy, beautiful and perfect and sun-lit, being visited by their subjects.

"I don't know what I'm gonna do without you for the next couple of weeks," Eric Woodard said, running his fingers through her loose curls. Leeda rolled over onto her stomach and propped herself up on her elbows to look at him. He was peering over his catalog at her, his dirty-blond hair messed up from lying on the ground. "Who's going to match my socks?"

Leeda smiled. She had an obsessive-compulsive habit of matching Eric's socks, which were all cashmere and sent by his mother. She also liked to fold anything that was hanging from anywhere. Leeda was very visual. She liked everything in her vision to be orderly.

"I'll be back before all your groupies know I'm gone and you can get a new girlfriend," she said. Eric rolled his eyes. Leeda liked to tease him about all the girls who constantly hit on him, sometimes right in front of her.

Leeda was headed home to Bridgewater, Georgia, for two weeks come Saturday. It was something she was ambivalent about. There were some things she was thrilled to see again after a whole year away. There were some things she would have been glad to skip. It seemed silly, but the hardest thing would be the two weeks without Eric.

They had met on the bus the first week of school. He had gotten her first name before he'd jumped off. Then he'd called the dean of her college and had made up some story to find out exactly who she was. When he'd showed up outside her second Tuesday econ class, Leeda had been wary. But Eric had assured her that once he set his mind to something he always followed through. He hadn't been lying. He had even known what he wanted to be since he was in fifth grade—a surgeon.

Tonight he'd make Leeda study with him like he always did. He liked to tease her that he was the reason she had an almost perfect GPA. But they both knew that wasn't true. Leeda didn't like Bs. They made her grade sheet look messy.

There were some ways, though, in which Eric had shaped her life at school. He knew everyone. He was always invited somewhere. He took to people like a swimmer takes to water, and he was always liked. It had been too easy for Leeda to ride his coattails into her group of friends at Columbia. She wasn't sure where she would have been without him in that aspect. She, too, was usually well liked. But not great at making close ties. She was too contained.

If there was such a thing as a white knight, Eric was hers. When he was around her, Leeda felt like she didn't have to worry about anything. It was something she couldn't explain. He was the kind of guy who took care of things. If there was anything she needed, she knew he would give it to her. It made her life feel as smooth as silk.

"You'll be batting off all those southern boys," he said, grinning up at her and also looking the tiniest bit worried.

Leeda rolled her eyes. "Yeah, you know how I'm into guys who drive tractors and drink Bud Light," she said. Murphy McGowen would have said she sounded snobby. But Eric didn't seem to notice.

He opened up the schedule book and showed it to her. "Here's the class I signed us up for."

Leeda read the description. Art of the Italian Renaissance. "That sounds good." It was a summer class Eric had talked her into. They planned to spend the rest of the summer sitting at sidewalk cafés, seeing movies, and taking advantage of all the city had to offer.

Leeda sometimes felt like her life as a Georgia girl had gone up in a puff of smoke, replaced by a New York life that was full of conversations about things that mattered and countless things to do. It had all surpassed her wildest expectations. On Fridays, she and Murphy had a permanent date, no matter who else tried to get in the way. Friday afternoons and evenings were theirs, without fail, to ride ferries, to tramp Fifth Avenue and window-shop, to ice-skate, to lie on the grass in Central Park, to eat falafel from stands, to get crepes in the East Village, to take up seats at diners for way too long while eating rice pudding, and sometimes just to stay cooped up in one of their dorm rooms and cowrite lively, chaotic e-mails to Birdie.

"What's the first thing you're gonna do when you get home?" Eric asked, scrunching up his eyebrows thoughtfully, his hazel eyes half caught in the shade Leeda cast. He had a smooth, open face, the kind you liked right away. Even his features were uncomplicated and honest.

Leeda's thoughts immediately went to the smell of peaches, which she had almost forgotten, and the Darlington Orchard. She had the same eager feeling about seeing it that a kid might get while anticipating going to Disney World, like it was something huge and far away. But in two days, she thought, it would be New York that felt far away and the orchard that would feel real—quaint and quiet and full of shadows and tucked away at what felt like the edge of the world. She didn't know how to explain her excitement to Eric, though. He was more of a facts and figures guy. "They're reading my grandmom Eugenie's will on Saturday. So I guess I'll do that."

Eric looked confused. "Didn't she . . . die a long time ago?"

"Yeah, last spring. The reading was supposed to be in the summer, but we all have to be there, and Danay and I have both been away." Leeda had spent Christmas with her sister, Danay, Danay's husband, and their parents in Jackson Hole, Wyoming, skiing and being civil to one another.

Leeda watched a group of girls walk across the grass, between them and a redbrick building where she had calculus.

"Do you think you'll inherit something interesting?" Eric asked. "I may need you to support me in med school."

Leeda smiled. They both knew he'd graduate near—if not at—the top of his class and get a scholarship. Even though his family was pretty well-off, and he didn't need one. "Grandmom was pretty wealthy, but Murphy says that if she left me anything, it will be doilies. Or maybe some coasters. She was really type A," Leeda joked. "She would want me to keep my glasses on coasters."

"Apple doesn't fall far from the Granny Smith tree."

Leeda shook her head furiously. "Oh no. I'm not like my grandmom."

"Was she defensive?" he teased, propping himself up on his elbows and playing with a bit of her hair, then leaning in to kiss her near her ear.

"Apparently," Leeda said, distracted by the question, considering it. "She got in a fistfight with my great-aunt once, because she told my grandmom she had handwriting like a boy."

"Ha!" Eric looked intensely interested. "She sounds wild."

Leeda thought of her grandmom, her minuscule frame, her tight white curls, her giant hats on Sundays. "Maybe when she was younger. When I knew her she was more stubborn than anything. And really conservative." Leeda twisted to face him more directly. "She wrote fan letters to Ronald Reagan."

He ran his hand across her cheek, just once, smiling. "Was she pretty like you?"

Leeda shrugged. She had looked kind of like a walnut by the time Leeda had known her.

"Who knows, maybe you'll inherit something surprising,"

Eric said, pulling a textbook out of the knapsack that Leeda had brought and handing it to her so she could study for her next exam.

Leeda wondered about what that something might be. Maybe she'd get more money than she'd thought, or less. Maybe she'd be slighted altogether. You never really knew with Grandmom Eugenie, who had been buried to the tune of "Blue Hawaii" and had owned a rescue shelter for miniature ponies.

If there was one thing her grandmom had been, besides conservative, it was contradictory, and that meant she was full of surprises.

Eric sighed. "Time to hit the books." He opened her book for her, happening on a page where she had stored a peach blossom and forgotten about it. It slid off the page and down into the grass.

"What's that?" he asked absently, pulling out a book of his own.

Leeda stared at it, touched its dry, paperlike petals, and smiled. "Just a flower," she said. "It's nothing important."

She brushed it aside and left it on the grass.

Two

*A*s usual, Birdie Darlington had her nose in a book.

Since coming to Mexico City to study at the National Autonomous University of Mexico for the year, Birdie had gotten hooked on travel books. Not for any practical purpose. She didn't plan to go to any of the places she was reading about. Flipping through pictures of strange lands was like a game to her, like flipping through catalogs and imagining what clothes she would buy if she had loads of money.

Growing up with the myth-loving, crystal-wearing Poopie Pedraza as her family's cook and surrogate second mom, Birdie saw magic in many things. Despite what she knew logically and factually, she imagined other countries much as people living a couple of hundred years ago might have—as an old map with lots left undiscovered. *Here, there be dragons.* It was because she had grown up on stories. She had grown up painting far-off lands in her own colors. And only Mexico City had been her litmus test. Indeed, it seemed to belong on a different planet. It felt like another kind of sun hung above her in Mexico. Birdie had never been more excited or enchanted, more stimulated or challenged, than she had this year while studying abroad. It was something she could take home with her.

Birdie planned to continue school at Florida State. She and Enrico Fiol, whom she'd followed here, would spend the summer together, stretching out their time as long as possible. Then she'd head back to the States, and real life, to get a degree in agriculture like she'd always planned. She and Enrico would make it work long-distance. And after school, Birdie would move home to take up her rightful place running her family's peach orchard. She planned one day to keep an old-fashioned collection of World Book Encyclopedias lined up on her shelf in the living room at home and to decorate her family's practically ancient farmhouse with colorful posters from Tahiti and China and Mozambique. Just because she would probably never go to the countries didn't mean she couldn't remind herself that they existed.

Her only regret was that she would have to say good-bye to Enrico at the end of the summer. And that she would miss a precious summer at home.

Bock bock bock.

A chicken, fat and white, its feathers a little disheveled from sleep, pecked at her shoelaces, distracting her.

"What do you want?" she asked, picking up Pollito and giving her a kiss on her head. Twice, Birdie had had to get lip medication from the doctor for a fungus she'd gotten from kissing her chicken. Over the phone, her mom had been furious. But Birdie couldn't help but kiss her chicken.

It had been easy to smuggle Pollito, (pronounced *Poyeeto*), whom she'd acquired on her first visit to Mexico City when

Enrico had rescued her from a chef, into her off-campus studio apartment. The place, perched on the top floor of a five-story building, was quiet and private, though it had barely enough space for Birdie and a chicken. It contained a small bedroom "area," a kitchenette that could be closed off with a folding door like a closet, a white tile floor, and a big gray suede chair.

It didn't help that Birdie's bedroom was full of clutter, albeit clutter that Birdie loved. A collection of wooden *santo*s lined the windowsill, over the heads of which she could see the Avenida de los Insurgentes and the rooftops of Mexico City beyond it. Photos of her butterfly-eared papillon dogs, Majestic and Honey Babe, standing side by side in argyle sweaters, and then a photo of Majestic alone, wearing a leg cast after Honey Babe had died, covered the wall. Masks and crazy little dolls she'd bought at the floating market; scarves so colorful they made your mouth water; matchbooks from her favorite restaurants; and photos of her, Leeda, and Murphy at the orchard lay strewn everywhere.

Birdie had set Pollito down and turned back to her book when there was a knock at the door. She placed the book on the arm of her chair and stood up, shuffling over in her slippers and pulling the door open carelessly, disheveled though she was, auburn hair flopping every which way, and wearing a sweatshirt she'd slept in and baggy khaki overalls. Enrico stood in the foyer.

"I brought pastries," he said, holding up a white paper bag, "and coffee with milk."

"*Café con leche*," Birdie said. They had a long-running argument over whether they should speak Spanish or English when they were together. Both wanted to practice.

Birdie sipped the coffee, thick with sweet condensed milk.

"Look at all the *café con leche* you keep bringing me," Birdie said, pinching a roll of fat on her stomach for Enrico to see.

Enrico smiled, pulled her in to kiss her on the cheek, and walked to the wall, looking at a new sketch Birdie had drawn. She was taking her first art class as an elective, and she loved it. It was a sketch, from memory, of Murphy's garden behind Birdie's house. A nectarine tree sloped over a gaggle of azaleas and a tangled patch of herbs.

"My parents want us over for dinner on Sunday," Enrico said. "Can you?"

Birdie shrugged. "Sure."

She loved going to Enrico's parents' house, about an hour out of the city. They planned to spend the summer there, which Murphy said was the weirdest thing she'd ever heard. But the Fiols treated Birdie like family. They even called her their daughter-in-law and cooked her favorite dishes. Their house had become her home away from home. For an often-homesick small-town girl, that was a big deal.

"Hey Pollito," Enrico said, bending over, lifting the chicken, and kissing her on the head. Enrico had gotten the chicken-kissing disease too. Birdie grinned, watching the two of them together, like they were all a little family.

"She's such a ham," Birdie said, referring to how Pollito had been acting ornery all morning, demanding attention. She had decided, soon into her relationship with her pet, that chickens had bigger personalities than anyone gave them credit for. Pollito, for instance, was gregarious, a little moody at times, and playful. Enrico, always sensitive and thoughtful, had decided to become a vegetarian almost as soon as they'd adopted her.

Because of her deep love for hamburgers, Birdie had taken a bit longer, but eventually she had converted too, especially after reading a book Enrico had given her about factory farming. Neither of them had told Poopie, who would certainly disapprove, despite all her new age sensibilities.

Enrico plopped down at the kitchen table, grabbed a book out of his backpack, and situated himself. He loved to read. He was a far more dedicated student than Birdie was, probably because he was far more cerebral. Right now, for instance, he was reading a book by Jorge Luis Borges that Birdie could hardly stand, even when she'd switched to the English translation. It was all brain games and too ethereal. Birdie was tactile. She was interested in things she could see and touch, or at least interested in reading about them.

Still, she plopped down too, reluctantly putting her travel book aside and, with a face full of angst—which made Enrico laugh—pulling out the book of South American political history she was supposed to be reading earlier.

"Do you have a highlighter?" she asked after a few moments, procrastinating. Enrico shook his head. She tried to focus again. "What about stickies?" She reached across the bed to where Enrico had left his backpack and unzipped the front pocket.

Enrico seemed lost in his book for a moment longer as she stuffed her hand into the pocket and her fingers brushed something small and square. But then he seemed to come to himself and jerked out of his chair. "Don't . . ." He moved toward her, but not before she had retrieved the object and pulled it out in front of her.

It was a little box. Small and blue and covered in felt. Birdie looked at it and then looked at him. She knew what it looked like. But she couldn't place it in the context of being in Enrico's bag or understand why he would have it.

"What is it?" she warbled.

His face flushed deeply.

"Is it for me?" Birdie whispered, feeling her stomach churn hotly.

Enrico didn't say anything. Even Pollito had gone deadly quiet.

Birdie turned it in her hands. It couldn't be. It was crazy to think it. But the weird silence made it feel possible.

Finally, Enrico reached out for the box. He sat beside her on the bed, bit his lip, looked at her, and then popped it open.

Birdie gasped.

There sat the tiniest, most delicate diamond ring. The three infinitesimal diamonds, descending diagonally like cherries, were like dots in a sea of tarnished silver backing. It looked old.

"Poopie gave it to me," he said. "She says it's been with the orchard since before they ever moved in. They found it sitting in the safe."

Birdie, ludicrously, felt like she could still pretend the ring wasn't what it was. "What's it for?" she asked.

"Birdie," Enrico said very earnestly, "I want to marry you."

Pollito let out a long series of *bock*s.

Birdie moved her hands so that she was sitting on top of them, just in case Enrico tried to slip the ring onto her finger.

"Um," she said. She saw the pastry bag sitting beside her on the bed. She reached for it and made a show of opening it casually, even though her hands were trembling. If she started eating, it would look like this wasn't a big deal, wouldn't it? It would look like Birdie got proposed to all the time or something. Or like she knew what she was doing. "Why?" she murmured through a mouthful of pastry. She asked it in a curious tone of voice, as if they were talking about why certain cavemen had been preserved so well over millions of years, or why the dollar was doing so poorly against the euro.

Enrico looked confused. Clearly it wasn't the reaction he had been hoping for.

"Um," he said. He sidled up next to her on the bed, turning the ring in his fingers. "Okay, um, well. I love you"—he flashed her a nervous smile that quickly disappeared as his face became very grave—"very much. And, you know, it's not so strange to get married young here, like it is in the U.S. And I want a promise to each other?" His voice rose uncertainly. "I think maybe it will make it easier when we are apart. Not . . ." He put his hand holding the box against her leg. Birdie jerked as if she were a vampire and the ring was a crucifix. "Not that I want to take away your freedom. But I thought . . . if you are happy with me, and I am happy with you . . ."

Birdie watched Enrico stumble along, her heart warming at his awkward little ways, the graveness of his face, and how clearly difficult this was for him.

Birdie was beginning to relax, and she was able to think. Her mom had run off with her dog Toonsis. Her dad had fallen in love with their cook. Birdie already came from a colorful family. Why on earth would they mind adding a teenage bride to the list?

She could think of a thousand reasons why they would mind. But the truth was, she couldn't imagine her future without

Enrico. She couldn't imagine someone who made her feel safer, or who made her laugh more, or who she was more comfortable with. All the times in Mexico City that she would have felt scared or out of place, Enrico had been there and had made everything feel familiar.

But most of all, Birdie felt like the answer was bigger than her, like it had to be the way it was, like it had already been decided somehow.

"I do," she said uncertainly. And then she remembered that was what you were supposed to say at the actual altar. "I mean, yes."

And finally she slid her hand toward him. She let Enrico take it and slip the ring onto her finger.

They both looked at her beringed hand as if it were an octopus or a sea monster. Some exotic, dangerous creature they had pulled from the deep.

In 1937, a young and beautiful Eugenie Cawley-Smith was seen sitting by the side of Orchard Road in her nightgown, crying. The three people who drove by her that morning—the trash collector; Mary Ann Gleason of Gleason Trim & Tailors; and Gertie Hinkle, who was unemployed—noticed that she was holding a piece of paper in her hands. They all thought it was odd, because she didn't like the orchard, she was recently—and by all accounts happily—married, and she never let anyone see her in her nightie.

Three

As the Greyhound bus idled in the cavernous depths of the Port Authority Bus Terminal, Murphy watched Leeda and her boyfriend hugging each other as if their ship were going down. Eric had his lips buried in Leeda's wavy blond hair and was saying something to her that Murphy couldn't hear. Murphy wanted to barf.

She plopped down on top of her upright suitcase and blinked at the ceiling, chewing on her pinky cuticle and tapping her feet. Finally the two pulled away from each other and shuffled toward her, holding hands and looking poetically melancholy.

"Oh, come on, she's not going off to World War I," Murphy said, standing up and wrapping her hand around her suitcase handle.

Eric smiled at her and patted the top of her curly head. "I'll miss you, Murphy."

Murphy rolled her eyes. Eric was one of Leeda's few friends who actually liked Murphy. Murphy didn't know why. She seemed to be the only person on earth who didn't like him back. Birdie said it was because Leeda gave him more attention than she gave Murphy. But Murphy didn't think so. It was something about how he was always going out of his way to make sure

Leeda didn't get her hair wet by carrying an umbrella over her, or how he always made sure Leeda didn't have to hail her own cabs. It was annoying.

"Can we get on the bus?" she asked in a fake-whiny voice.

"Hey, did you bring any snacks?" Leeda asked. "I'm hungry."

Murphy sighed theatrically and knelt down on the dirty concrete sidewalk, upending her suitcase and opening it to pull out a bag of soggy cheese fries she'd been saving for later. She handed them to Leeda, who studied the contents of the bag with a wrinkled, frightened look.

"You put a bag of cheese fries in your suitcase?" she asked, looking over at the suitcase's other contents. Murphy's clothes were bulging out in a messy heap.

"They're in a bag," Murphy said.

Leeda was simply shaking her head when her BlackBerry rang, distracting her. Murphy breathed a sigh of relief. Leeda probably would have tried to fold her clothes.

Leeda put her ear to the phone and smiled at Murphy to let her know it was Birdie on the phone. "Uh-huh . . . uh-huh . . . uh-huh." She nodded. "Well, Bird, if that's what you want it to be . . . Yeah . . . yeah, sure . . ."

Birdie had called five times since yesterday. First with the shocking news that she was engaged. Then, before either of them could really process the information or even accept that it was real, she'd called with several ideas about how many kids she wanted and would Enrico want the same number, and then with a long treatise about how she hoped her antique ring wasn't a blood diamond and should she take it somewhere to have it analyzed about that, and if it did turn out to be one should she cash it in and send money to Africa, and if so how would she decide which country to donate the money to?

Eric looked at Murphy as if he wanted to make conversation, but Murphy turned and pretended to study a piece of gum on the ground. She was in an agitated mood, more agitated than usual. She had spent the morning cleaning out her in-box on her Yahoo! account—moving things to folders, trying to get ready for a clean start come next year. She wouldn't have much access to a computer this summer while living at her mom's lavish estate at Anthill Acres Trailer Park.

There had been e-mails in there she hadn't opened and didn't know what to do with. She had shoved them into a folder she'd labeled *Blah Blah Blah* and had decided to forget about them. But she hadn't forgotten.

It really wasn't like Murphy. She wasn't a nostalgic person or a pack rat. Her mom, Jodee, had sent her to Bible school once for a whole summer. There, Murphy had learned the story of the sinful cities of Sodom and Gomorrah. A guy named Lot and his wife weren't so sinful as the rest. They were told to flee and never to look back. But on the way out, Lot's wife hadn't been able to resist a little peek, and she was turned into a pillar of salt. The only impression the story had made on Murphy was that Lot's wife was a chump. Looking back was the last thing she would ever be tempted to do.

Leeda crisply stuck her BlackBerry back in her pocket. Standing there with her Burberry luggage, her Stella McCartney jacket, and her perfect hair, she looked like the kind of person who owned New York. If Murphy hadn't known her, she would have disliked her on sight.

"Oh." Leeda looked like she'd forgotten something. "Sorry, Murphy, she didn't ask to talk to you."

"That's okay. I think my ear will fall off if I hear the words *Sierra Leone* one more time."

They stood in silence for a moment, watching the bus fill up. Then Leeda fidgeted, brushing Murphy's unruly, curly hair off where it had landed on her back. "Your hair is like a spider."

"I can't help it. It's vibrant."

Finally, after the passengers had trickled on board, they were the only people left on the platform. Murphy pulled her suitcase forward and Leeda, hanging back to say a final good-bye to Eric, followed. They plopped into two seats in the middle of the bus. A moment later they lurched into motion. Leeda waved out the window and then they turned the corner and joined the Manhattan traffic. Murphy watched the buildings, shops, and sidewalks go by.

"How did Birdie sound?"

"Far away."

"Like she was in Mexico?"

Leeda smiled. "Yeah."

As they approached Thirty-fourth Street, Murphy looked at Leeda. Leeda could afford to fly home. But instead she'd opted to sit with Murphy through a fourteen-hour bus ride. Murphy felt badly that she hadn't thanked her yet.

"I hope you and that guy don't get married," she said instead, because she wasn't great at thank-yous. "It would set evolution too far forward. Your baby would be better looking than that Brad Pitt kid, Moses or Shiloh or whatever. Hard on the rest of us tadpoles."

Leeda rolled her eyes. "Yeah, and your babies would be total slouches." When the two were out together, it was Murphy who had the freakish ability to make random guys approach her out of nowhere. Once she had been hit on by a Hare Krishna while they were eating ice cream in the East Village. She could bend spoons with the sheer force of her curves. "Do you ever want a boyfriend again?" Leeda mused.

"I have boyfriends."

"You have boys. Not boyfriends. Heartbreaker."

Murphy shrugged, lifting her hands and staring at her nails jokingly. "One seems boring."

Leeda nodded, taking it in. She was quiet for a moment. She looked like she wanted to ask something but didn't want to look like it was a big deal. "Does Rex know when you're coming home?"

Murphy let out a breath and shook her head.

Of all the guys Murphy had kissed—and there were a lot—Rex was her only ex. Murphy had always liked to play with boys, as if they didn't go any deeper than their tattoos or the music they liked or their haircuts. Rex had been different. He had loved her, was the thing. She had loved him.

Murphy whipped out her MP3 player and plugged in her earphones, giving Leeda one of the buds even though Leeda hated her music. They watched New York disappear as the Lincoln Tunnel engulfed them.

Murphy only liked to sleep when there was nothing going on that couldn't be missed. She stored up sleep time for rainy days. So when she slept, she slept hard.

As soon as they hit New Jersey, she drifted off, and she didn't wake up again until a bathroom break in Maryland. The next time she woke, it was getting dark and they were in North Carolina, on a featureless stretch of flat, tree-lined road, unidentifiable except for the signs announcing upcoming towns. She and Leeda played hearts for a couple of hours, stared out the window for a while, and then went back to sleep. When Murphy woke for good, they were just passing the sign for the town of Dobney, National Home of Cheese Grits.

"Birdie loves those cheese grits," Leeda said wistfully. "It'll be so weird being home without her."

Murphy's stomach began a slow jelly roll into a tight knot. She hadn't thought about what would happen once they got off the bus—as if the bus were a tiny country and they were going to live in it forever. Now that they'd reached the home of cheese grits, the town of Bridgewater felt imminent, robbing her of that feeling of insulation.

Murphy sat forward, agitated. "What time is it?" she asked, staring into the dark night.

"It's about one-thirty," Leeda said.

Murphy's feet began to tingle restlessly. She chewed at her thumbnail. Her stomach lurched with a strange excitement as the bus slowed down and turned off the exit toward town. The driver opened the door to let in some air now that the bus had slowed. The springy night air came rushing in, full of the smell of trees, white dirt, and warm tar. The soft wind blew back the passengers' hair.

Everything went from featureless to familiar. Places Murphy had seen countless times—what seemed like a million years ago—drifted by. Bob's Big Boy, the windows dark. A Dollar Star she had stolen underwear from. The KFC she used to wing water balloons at from the woods when one of the guys she was dating worked there.

The annoying thing was, Murphy had lived in Bridgewater for eighteen years. She had only known Rex for one of them, and still, layered on top of all the other memories were thoughts of Rex and her riding bikes, Rex and her eating lunch in this parking lot or sitting on that bench in front of Wendy's. It caught her by surprise.

She thought of the e-mails in the *Blah Blah Blah* folder with a sick thud. There were over thirty of them, all from Rex. And she hadn't read a single one. From the moment she'd left home she had ignored him completely, cut him off, left him out.

It hadn't really occurred to her, until just now, that when she saw him she wouldn't know how to explain herself. And he would probably find that hard to forgive. Maybe impossible.

Four

Mexico City had nowhere quiet to walk. It was one of the few things Birdie really disliked about it. Everywhere you went there were people and buildings, always accompanied by noise. For someone who'd learned to sort through her thoughts by walking under drooping pecan trees and into quiet shady corners, it could be hard to focus when she needed to.

Today Birdie was walking aimlessly in the city's center. She had just finished her last final. Enrico was waiting for her to come over so they could head to an engagement party being thrown for them by one of their friends. But Birdie's feet had led her away from his dorm building and down by the floating market, then past the bus station, winding along the streets, people watching. She kept circling back to a particular pay phone, staring at it, biting her pinky nail absently, and walking away. She didn't *need* to call anyone. She just kept feeling like she *had* to call someone. Finally she picked up the receiver, fished her phone card out of her wallet, and began to dial.

"Hello?" Murphy's sleepy voice came over the other end of

the line. Georgia was two hours ahead, but Murphy had never been an early riser. Birdie was grateful she had even picked up.

"Murphy?"

"Bird? You okay?" Murphy croaked, slowly waking up.

"Yeah. I just . . . wanted to know how your trip went."

"Fine," Murphy murmured. "It's weird being home."

"I bet," Birdie warbled. She didn't know why, but hearing Murphy at home in Georgia set her on the verge of tears. A few feet in front of her, a man spit on the sidewalk. Sometimes she hated Mexico City.

"What's going on, Bird?"

Birdie hesitated. She didn't know what to say. She kicked her toes against the concrete beneath her, staring at a piece of flattened gum stuck there.

In the days since Enrico had proposed, Birdie had gone from nervous to giddy to something else entirely. Some feeling she didn't recognize. And the more she'd tried to swallow it and write it off, the bigger it had gotten. It was close to the feeling of forgetting something.

"Nothing. I just can't believe I'm not gonna be there with you guys this summer."

"I know. Me too. It's the worst."

They were quiet for a while, missing each other. A woman had arrived at the phone booth and had dropped two big satchels of vegetables. She hovered, looking at Birdie directly to let her know she was waiting.

"So are you still engaged today?"

Birdie laughed softly. "Yeah."

"You sound, I dunno. You sound weird."

Birdie could hear that Murphy was perfectly awake now. And it felt like a blessing that, when Murphy was awake, she noticed everything, and then she called you out on it.

"I . . . I don't know if I can explain it. . . ." She studied her brown Teva sandals instead, then looked at the lady waiting for the phone. Birdie was growing a little self-conscious.

"Try, Birdie."

Birdie kicked her feet gently against the pavement. "I just, you know what? I feel really angry."

"Why?"

Birdie considered.

"I'm angry because . . . because Enrico has floppy hands. And he wears these nubby white pants. I hate white pants. I just stare at him in those white pants and I want to—"

"What?"

"I don't want to say."

"Birdie . . ."

"Okay. I just want to punch him in the face."

Murphy guffawed and then immediately silenced herself.

"What do you think?" Birdie asked.

"You know what I think."

Murphy had already said she thought Birdie wasn't ready to be engaged. A lot of people would have said that. But Birdie was excited to have this thing with Enrico. She was excited that she could have him around for the rest of her life. She couldn't imagine finding someone better to make a life with.

"I'm not like you, Murphy. I don't need to sow my wild oats like you do. I like being settled."

"But maybe you're settling. Maybe that's what you're feeling.

Remember that time you were telling me about Disney World? How you said you really loved the Dumbo ride?"

"Yeah."

"Okay, well, so you said you didn't want to go on any other ride, but then you went on Space Mountain. And well, you know, that ride is way better."

"Enrico is not the Dumbo ride!" Birdie gasped into the phone.

"Okay, okay," Murphy said sheepishly. "Then I don't know. I don't know what's going on with your feelings. You're a deep well, Birdie. Things take a while to play out with you sometimes."

Birdie fiddled with the phone cord. She felt badly for yelling at Murphy, who knew her so well.

"I feel scared."

"That, I understand," Murphy murmured.

"I feel like I've forgotten something big."

They both were silent for a while. Birdie let out a wistful sigh. She decided to change the subject.

"Are you gonna see Rex?" she asked.

"Oh, maybe. I dunno."

Birdie smiled. Murphy acted the most careless about the things that made her the most nervous.

A voice interrupted them in Spanish, telling them they had one minute left.

"Okay, well," Birdie said, "I guess I'm out of credit on my phone card. And some lady's waiting to use the phone anyway."

"Okay. Okay. Well, I hate that you're not here. You're not still kissing that stupid chicken, are you?"

"No," Birdie lied.

"All right. Love you."

"You too."

Birdie hung up the phone and stared at it for a minute. Then she turned and walked.

She walked back the way she'd come, down by the floating market, and into a stationery store. She bought some paper, an envelope, and stamps, and then walked back outside, positioning herself on a stone bench.

She thought maybe she'd write to her mom. Or maybe to Poopie. It was still weird, sometimes, choosing between them in little ways like this.

But finally she decided that what was inside was too big to write to either of them. She just stared off into space, tapping the pen against her chin, miserable.

She decided to write a fake letter instead.

Enrico, she wrote. *I can't do this. Please forget me.*

She felt tears welling up in her eyes at her own melodramatic words. But they calmed her. It was like shock therapy. They were things she'd never actually say or mean. She tapped the pen against her chin for a moment.

Your white pants make me want to punch you in the face.

Birdie

Birdie stared at the letter and a tiny, peaceful smile slipped onto her face. She took it a step further, tearing off a stamp, licking it, and placing it on the front of the envelope. For the return address she wrote, *Birdie, Country Mouse.*

And then she stood up and started walking again.

She walked past the bus station, but this time she stopped, staring at a bus with the banner AEROPUERTO.

She longed to go to the *aeropuerto*. She longed to hop a flight and go home and forget that Mexico and Enrico had ever happened. Then she wouldn't have to make choices.

There was a blue postbox right by the ticket counter. Birdie stared at her letter, feeling half crazy. She wouldn't send it, of course.

But she found herself walking to the postbox. She found herself opening the tiny door. She found herself laying the letter upon it, tempting fate.

And then, with the recklessness of someone who has kissed chickens and flown off to study in foreign lands, she dropped it in.

Five

Murphy stretched in bed, staring at the dingy white ceiling overhead. Her tiny window looked out on the patchy dead grass behind Anthill Acres Trailer Park. She could smell the coffee and microwave dinners that had saturated the trailer over the years. It was like a museum of her former life.

She rolled sideways out of bed and slunk out through the skinny door into the living room where her mom was bent over the table reading the paper, coffee in one hand. She looked over and beamed at Murphy.

Murphy hugged her from behind and then flung herself down on the couch. She blinked at the table for a few minutes, waking up. The night before, they'd barely caught up before Jodee had gone back to bed. Murphy had stayed up watching TV, unable to sleep after hibernating on the bus. Her mom handed her a coffee.

"I'll get another cup." She stood.

Murphy and her mom had lived in Anthill Acres all Murphy's life, and her mom had lived in Bridgewater since dinosaurs had roamed the earth. Jodee had grown up two blocks down the street in a house that was now a shell, overgrown with kudzu.

"What's new?" Murphy asked. By the look of things, the answer was nothing.

Jodee looked at the TV, picking at her fingernails. "Oh, you know. Work's good."

Murphy studied her. She had expected her mom to gush. Jodee usually loved having someone to talk to. But this morning, she was quiet, reserved, a little strange.

"Dating anyone?" Murphy asked, trying to jump-start the conversation.

She shook her head. "Nope." Jodee smiled at her and took her hand. "Oh, sweetie, I'm glad you're home," she drawled.

"Me too." At the moment, sitting with her mom, she really meant it. She squinted at Jodee. "Is everything okay?"

Jodee nodded brightly.

Murphy asked after people in town. Two of her classmates had gotten married. Cynthia Darlington's teahouse was doing well. Judge Miller Abbott's wife had died. But soon Jodee fell into an odd, awkward silence and fidgeted in her seat.

Frustrated, Murphy thrust herself out of her chair. "I think I'm gonna go over to the orchard," she said. "See Poopie and Walter."

"That sounds nice."

Murphy assessed her mom with one last glance, then walked into her bedroom and pulled on long shorts and an orange tank top. She corralled her defiant dark curls into some kind of frizzy ponytail. She grabbed her knapsack and headed out the door.

Outside, she unlocked her bike and hopped on. She pulled out to the edge of the parking lot.

But instead of turning left, up Orchard Road, she guided her handlebars to the right.

She rode toward town, taking in the sights. It all felt surreal to Murphy, like something far away, but also exactly the same as the day she'd left. Main Street felt like a time warp. She rode past the courthouse, where she'd stood in front of the judge at least twenty times for various acts of rebelliousness. She rode past Rex's dad's hardware store. Here, she paused her bike for a moment, confused. Though the store looked the same, the familiar sign hanging above the door had been replaced by an Ace Hardware sign.

"Hmm." She sighed. She kicked her bike back into motion. Past the cemetery.

As she got closer to Rex's, she began to bike slower, zigzagging over the bridge, studying the trees and the flowers and thinking about turning around. Murphy went over some rules with herself. She wouldn't act too happy to see him—that would lead him on. She wouldn't apologize for not replying to his e-mails—she still stood by her decision that it had been the right thing to do. Why should she feel obligated to hold on to something that didn't work for her anymore?

Murphy took a deep breath. It was a beautiful spring day. The river under the bridge was usually dried up, but today it was an even trickle. The sound of the water was hypnotizing.

She turned off the bridge and onto Rex's street, edging the cemetery. She could see a corner of his gray one-story prefab house peeking out through the trees ahead. Her pulse picked up a little.

Pedaling the bike as slowly as it could possibly go without

falling over, she wound out from the cover of the trees. And then she stopped, her sneakers hitting the pavement at the edge of the driveway. The gravel was dotted with about fifteen old newspapers, some of them turning back to mush. The lights were out.

She pulled in and parked her bike, hovering over the kickstand longer than she needed to. She walked up the stairs onto the front porch and pushed the porch swing next to her with her foot, staring at it for a few moments, watching it move back and forth, forward and back, a pain rising in her chest. Finally she stopped it with her hand and walked to the window behind it, pressing her face up against the glass. She peered inside at the house. The furniture, the curtains, the radio that Rex's dad had liked to listen to, the oil painting of ducks above the couch, even the washer and dryer . . .

Gone.

Six

Outside the banquet room of the Cawley-Smith Hotel, the late May breeze was lifting the leaves, but no one had bothered to open a window.

Leeda sat back in her chair and stared at the gently waving branches. Next to her, her sister, Danay, leaned forward casually, her hair fanning over her right shoulder. In front of Leeda, on the table, was a paperweight with the Cawley-Smith logo on it. Leeda ran her fingers over its cool glass.

At the head of the table, Grandmom Eugenie's lawyer shuffled papers. He was also the lawyer of the entire Cawley-Smith family and half the well-heeled people in town—which added up to about twenty, including the heiress to a local ginger ale fortune and a family whose predecessor had invented and patented a new way to process pork cracklings.

Fourteen people had showed up for the reading of the will. Grandmom Eugenie's money and influence had stretched like tentacles all over the town of Bridgewater. She had been partial owner of the family bed-and-breakfast, as well as benefactress for various charities—such as the Kings County Miniature Pony

Rescue and the Pecan Trail Tourism Committee. On top of that, no one would have been surprised if she'd had gold doubloons buried in a cookie tin in her backyard. People had come with less hope of getting a lot of money than of seeing a show.

"Talk to your uncle Gabe after this," Leeda's mom, sitting to her left, whispered to her. "He said he'd give you some advice on building up your résumé for business school."

"Mom, I'm a freshman."

"It's never too early. Danay started laying the groundwork for her law degree as soon as she got to school."

Leeda looked over at her sister, happily chatting with one of their aunts. She was wearing a short-sleeve, impeccably tailored maroon suit, and her long straight hair was combed down her back. Danay seemed happily at ease wherever she was, and today was no exception.

Being home was already getting to Leeda. She felt dwarfed next to the person she thought she was in New York—fun, sort of cool and glamorous, together. Being around her family made her feel aimless and sort of lame. She felt like someone else around them, but she didn't know whom.

Her dad had picked her up from the bus stop the night before, hugged her briefly, and asked her lots of questions about the weather in New York on the ride home. She hadn't seen her mom until this morning, and although Leeda had felt full of things to tell about her life in the city, she hadn't been able to think of much to say. There was something awkward about being loving in the Cawley-Smith family. Leeda sometimes felt as though they were all intimate strangers. It gave her a sinking feeling, now that she was back.

Finally the lawyer cleared his throat and tapped his papers to straighten them. The low murmur of the room quieted as he launched into a lengthy, monotonous reading of all the legal preliminaries. Leeda quickly started to zone out, looking out the window at the trees again, longing to find Murphy, head to the orchard and see Poopie and her uncle Walter, and lie in the grass.

She was attentive enough to hear that Eugenie had left her house, Primrose Cottage, to her mom, to be either kept or sold as Lucretia wished once a home had been found for the miniature ponies in the corral in the backyard.

The lawyer continued down the list of parcels of money and other pieces of property that had been left to Leeda's uncles and aunts.

"To my granddaughters, I leave the following—" Leeda turned, hoping now that it was doilies, so she and Murphy could have a good laugh. "To Danay, I leave my shares in the Cawley-Smith Hotels, accessible at her discretion."

Leeda glanced at Danay. She looked surprised and pleased. It seemed weird, being happy about something you got because someone had died. Leeda scratched the back of her neck, feeling self-conscious.

"To Leeda, I leave the sum of five hundred thousand dollars . . ."

Leeda was sure she had misheard. But the way the room suddenly clammed up made her heart skip a beat. Her eyes found their way first to Danay's bewildered ones and then to her mother's look of shock. The lawyer continued. ". . . upon the following condition. Leeda will undertake the stewardship of my Kings County Miniature Pony Rescue. The ponies are currently under the care of a worker I have retained for them. Leeda will need to find a home, or homes, for the ponies." From her right, Leeda could hear one of the onlookers snort, but she was too dazed to see who. Some people snickered under their breath. "The money is intended to be more than enough for the care of my babies. However, once the ponies are properly cared for, Leeda is free to do with the remaining money as she wishes.

"She should take up residence at Primrose Cottage until she has finished dispensing her duties, at which time the house will be transferred to her mother. Failure to accept this responsibility will render Leeda's inheritance void, and the money will go to a charity I have specified." The lawyer seemed reluctant to go on, but then sheepishly continued reading. "If my ponies are not looked after properly, you can bet I will be frowning down on you from the hereafter."

A few giggles rang out in the group. It was the Eugenie they'd come for.

Leeda sat stock-still. As if sitting stock-still could mean that twenty-three ponies would run right past her, on to the next corral.

Mandie Rae Adlai arrived in Bridgewater on a summer night in 1928, riding a horse and holding a contract in her hand stating that she'd won the Darlington Peach Orchard in a poker game. She was wildly beautiful and unattached, and the rumors arrived almost as soon as she did. Some said she was a widow. Some said she was a witch. And though seven men came to court her before she skipped town nine years later, she never had eyes for any of them.

Seven

Murphy climbed off her bike at the foot of the driveway that led up to the Darlington Orchard. A figure was standing there, kicking pebbles aimlessly.

Murphy pulled off her sweatshirt and tied it around her waist.

"What are you doing? Loitering?" Murphy asked. Leeda continued her listless game of gravel soccer.

"I had my mom drop me off. But . . ." She stared up the driveway. ". . . then I didn't want to go in. It feels like trespassing without Birdie here."

"Don't be ridiculous." This was one of the areas where she and Leeda differed. Murphy felt at home everywhere. Leeda held herself at a polite distance.

"How long have you been here?" Murphy asked.

"An hour."

"An hour," Murphy echoed.

Leeda shrugged her thin shoulders. She held herself so erect that it was easy to forget her tininess. Her bones were like bird's bones. But sometimes, like right now, it struck Murphy just how fragile Leeda could seem.

"Come on." Murphy grabbed her around the elbow and Leeda softened like a rag doll, letting herself be dragged.

As they walked up the drive, their sneakers crunched in the gravel and echoed in the quiet. The orchard unveiled itself slowly as they walked. There was a slightly sunken barn to their right, the great doors closed and the red paint peeling. Beyond it, the peach trees began, poking out of the white sandy ground in an orderly, checkered pattern, only their crooked, gnarled branches wild and unkempt. The peaches, abundantly nestled in their leaves, were fully grown, but they had a greenish tinge to them, with just a pale blush covering each one in soft pink. Bobwhites and finches were flitting in and out of some of the branches and through the rows. There was a rapping somewhere far away, probably a woodpecker. And lots of buzzing.

"Not ripe yet," Murphy said.

"Second week of June," Leeda replied. They knew it all by heart—which varieties ripened when, even which trees ripened faster than others because of where they sat: on a hill, in a dip, in fuller sun, closer to water. Murphy had forgotten what so much green looked like and how alive everything felt. Life even had a smell. Flowers and grass and the smell of wood.

The driveway curved and the white clapboard workers' dorms emerged into view on the left—the new women's dorm, which had been built that year, gleaming whiter and standing straighter than the older, crooked men's dorm. In the center was a dusty clearing with a large black grill and a circle of logs sur- rounding a fire pit.

To the right, the house sprawled across a bright green lawn. The Darlingtons' house seemed to pin the whole place down and hold it together. It was the heart of the property, old and huge and rambling, with sleepy windows and a wide front porch that the girls had spent countless afternoons lounging on. Just looking at a house like the Darlingtons' reminded people of old things and made them wonder how long that banister had been crooked, who had painted the shutters, and how many people had lived there.

Murphy gazed around. It all felt eerily empty. No workers in the fields or in the dorms. No fires burning and none of Poopie's music floating out from the windows of the house. Murphy nudged her bike onto its kickstand, and the girls crossed the lawn in great strides. They climbed the sagging stairs onto the front porch, the wood underneath their feet creaking with each step.

"It doesn't look like anyone's home," Leeda said. Murphy tried the door, which was locked. Even when Walter and Poopie were out, they usually left the door open.

Murphy looked back to check again that Walter's truck was in the driveway, then she pushed the little glass doorbell. Leeda pressed her face against the big window next to the door, cupping her hands at either side of her face.

"Did they skip town?" she asked, her breath fogging the glass.

"Crazy lovebirds." Murphy breathed. Maybe Poopie and Walter had thrown caution to the wind and had gone off gallivanting on a romantic adventure.

Sticking her hands in the pockets of her jeans, Murphy turned to gaze at the view from the porch. The peach trees crept up to the opposite edge of the sprawling lawn, pygmylike, as if they were going to launch a surprise assault on the house. A cool breeze lifted her hair, and she moved to sink down on the top step, out from under the porch roof, where the sun could warm her. It was one of those spring days where the shade could cause shivers and the sun could make a girl warm and lazy like a cat. Just sitting here on the Darlingtons' front porch dulled the picture of Rex's empty house in her head.

Leeda sat down beside her and leaned back on her palms, tapping her heels against the stairs. "It's really good to be here," she said.

Murphy looked at her quizzically. "Hey, how was the will reading?"

Leeda sighed, still staring out at the trees. "I inherited the ponies."

Murphy let out a guffaw. "The minis? The My Little Ponys?"

"And half a million dollars."

Murphy stopped mid-guffaw.

Leeda finally looked over at her.

"Oh my God." Murphy leaned forward, excitedly gripping the stairs behind her. "What are you going to do?"

Leeda shrugged. "Well, spend some of it on the ponies until I find a home for them. Invest the rest, I guess. That's what my uncle says to do."

"Leeda, your life is so easy. Do you know how many people work their whole lives and don't make that kind of money?"

Leeda nodded absently. "It feels like a big responsibility." She sighed. "I guess it shouldn't take more than a couple weeks to find homes for the ponies. But I still want to make my flight to New York on the seventh."

"I hope Mitzie doesn't get too attached to you," Murphy teased. She had long been amused by the miniature pony rescue and the long line of older ladies who held fund-raising lunch-eons for it in town. Mitzie was the poster pony, and a banner of her hung on the side of the Bridgewater Community Bank proclaiming MITZIE NEEDS YOUR HELP.

Leeda laughed.

Murphy studied her. Even with the ridiculous announcement about the ponies and the astounding one about the half a million dollars, Leeda's face was blank and inscrutable. More than any-one else, Leeda was often a mystery to Murphy, despite her knowing Leeda and Birdie better than anyone. Sometimes she could look at Leeda and have no clue what she might be feeling, where she might be heading.

"Hey," Leeda said, suddenly brightening, as if she were remembering something important. "Did you see Rex?"

Murphy stood, climbed down the rest of the steps, and stretched out on the grass—the strong, itchy, organic smell of it filling her nostrils, the tiny blades scratching at her bare arms, the lump of her sweatshirt bunched up underneath her.

"I'm a dead body," she said.

Leeda kneeled next to her, feeling her pulse.

"What killed you?"

Murphy rolled over onto her side, looked at her, over her. "Let's go for a walk."

Leeda pulled her up by the wrists.

They crossed the lawn and the driveway and walked down to the stately pecan grove, then along the fence that separated the orchard from the pristine and manicured lawn of the Balmeade Country Club, their feet crunching and rolling on old fallen nuts. In the two years Murphy had been truly familiar with the orchard, it had survived a hurricane, a dorm fire, and Horatio Balmeade's attempts to buy it in order to expand his property. Where the Darlington and Balmeade properties met was like night and day—chaotic and overgrown and lush on the orchard side, pristine and sterile and impeccably groomed on the country club side.

They trailed along the fence, walking up behind the dorms and down the path that led to the garden Murphy had adopted.

Here, they stopped, staring around, shocked.

The garden, when they had left it, had been a large patch of flowers nestled in its own space between the trees. Now the only visible signs that it had been there at all were the wooden bench Rex had made for Murphy two summers before and an adolescent nectarine tree. The garden was teeming with kudzu, strangler vines, and tall weeds. Everything else—the roses, the peonies, the butterfly bushes, the herb garden—had been overrun.

Murphy could feel Leeda looking at her. Murphy looked at the remnants of her plants, abandoned to early deaths.

"I'm a drifter, baby," she murmured. She didn't want to linger. She turned on her heel, and Leeda followed her back down the trail.

Their spirits dampened, they made their way toward the lake, disappearing into the peach rows and letting their fingers loll along the dangly green leaves as they walked. The leaves were shaped like skinny feathers. Murphy picked a few half-ripe peaches and pegged them at Leeda's back. The places where she'd snapped them from the trees gave off a sour, green odor. Leeda waggled her arms behind her.

They were just approaching the clearing up ahead, the trees

growing thinner, when they heard the soft rumble of a car coming up the driveway.

Leeda grinned. "They're back."

They turned in the direction they'd come and started to jog.

A cab was stopped at the top of the drive, idling while the fare was paid. Leeda and Murphy were nearly halfway across the grass when the door opened. But neither Walter nor Poopie got out.

Only one figure emerged from the cab, looking crumpled and hunched and forlorn.

Leeda and Murphy froze like statues, too surprised to move.

They would have known that teddy-bear suitcase anywhere.

Eight

It was as if the whole year disappeared the moment she set foot on the grass. Birdie took a deep breath and sank into her friends' embraces. It was like letting out a breath she hadn't known she'd been holding. She was back in her comfort zone. Back where everyone spoke her language and shared her past and everything was easy.

"What happened?"

"What are you doing here?"

Birdie smiled. She felt like she'd been through a long, difficult journey and had arrived at the peaceful oasis. Behind it all lurked the nagging, horrible feeling that she'd just done something she hadn't meant to do. But right now, she didn't care. Home was like a blanket wrapping her up. It made everything else okay.

"Everything's fine," she said. She would tell them about Enrico as soon as she got settled. First, she just had to bask. She stared at her friends. Leeda's face had thinned a little, become a little more fine and sculpted at the cheekbones. Her hair had grown to just below her shoulders, and she had lost her freckles again, her face white and smooth as fine china. Murphy too had gotten a little thinner, but it only seemed to accentuate her curvy frame. She was wearing a green T-shirt with a silk-screened image of a sax on the front, her hands in her pockets. She looked utterly relaxed.

Birdie looked toward the parking lot, then up at the house.

"Are Poopie and my dad here?"

"No," Murphy said. "We came to see them, but the house is empty."

Birdie looked up at the house, perplexed.

But as if on cue, there was the sound of a car coming up the driveway, and they all turned. A second taxi, probably the second taxi to have ever come to Darlington Orchard, was coming toward them. Poopie, seeing the girls, had rolled down the window to wave, and when she caught sight of Birdie, she had the door open in a moment, hopping out before the driver could stop.

The reunion was chaotic and joyful. Poopie, always emotional, shed a couple of tears. Walter, Birdie's dad, was stoic but clearly delighted as he stepped out of the taxi.

"What are you doing here?" he asked, giving her a strong hug. Walter was tall, white haired, and broad shouldered. He was in blue jeans and a button-down short-sleeve shirt. He towered over the petite, brown-skinned Poopie. But Poopie dominated him with her expressiveness—her eyes wide, her hands moving in big loops as she *ooh*ed and *aah*ed over Birdie.

"I am making sure you are real," she said, feeling Birdie's arms, cupping her cheeks with her hands. "How are you here?"

"I just wanted to spend the summer at home," Birdie said, relaxed and relieved and safe. That was when she noticed the hat shaped like an alligator sticking out of Poopie's big black sack of a purse.

"Were you guys in Florida?" she asked.

Poopie and Walter gave each other significant looks. "Yes," Poopie said. "Well, we can talk about it inside. Come on."

Inside, they all gathered around the table in the Darlingtons' seventies-style kitchen, where the floor dipped in the middle and the yellowed counters had scorch marks and chips. The stairs across the hallway that ascended from the edge of the kitchen to the upstairs were crooked and listed to one side. Murphy called it "The Fun House."

"This tastes amazing," Murphy said. They'd all gotten situated with some bread, which Poopie had made and frozen, and peach-blackberry preserves left over from last year. The house was quiet without Majestic. When Birdie had asked where she was, her dad had explained that they still needed to go get her from the kennel.

"You going to pick peaches for us this year, Murphy?" Walter asked, sopping up some jam with his toasted bread. Poopie turned to Murphy too.

Murphy nodded. "Yeah, I was hoping. . . ."

Walter smiled. "We'd love to have you. You can stay in the dorms again if you want. We'll even give you a raise."

Murphy grinned. They hadn't paid her the year before. She'd been forced into it, at first, as a summer punishment.

Birdie looked at Leeda, who was conspicuously silent, rubbing her fingers against the edge of the table. Birdie wondered if she felt left out.

"We could use you too, Leeda," Poopie offered, "until you have to go."

Leeda brightened a bit.

"So where were you guys?" Birdie asked, feeling a strange sense of wariness. She wasn't sure if it was just that she felt weird about her dad and Poopie going away together, or that she felt protective of her mom. Not that her mom cared. It had been she who'd left Birdie's dad almost three years ago, not the other way around. Birdie glanced at the phone. She'd need to call her soon and tell her she was home.

Poopie and her father were looking at each other again significantly. "We went to look at houses," Walter said.

Birdie cocked her head and squinted at them. Her first reaction was simply to think it was funny and weird that they'd go on a trip to look at houses. "Why?"

Her dad folded his hands on the table. "Well, we had the property appraiser out a few months ago, and the foundations are in bad shape. With the caves running under the property, it's a big mess. The ground's too soft, and the house has sunk too far."

Birdie had always known about the caves running under the farm. Sometimes, when it was dead quiet in the kitchen, she swore she could hear the sound of trickling water echoing somewhere far beneath her.

Birdie looked to Poopie, confused.

"We are selling," Poopie said.

Birdie felt a bunch of tiny bits inside her start to throb and move and itch. Beside her, she felt Leeda and Murphy go completely still.

"But . . ." The first thing that occurred to Birdie was that her dad couldn't have thought it all through. The decision had to have been made on a whim. The Darlingtons had fought tooth and nail for much of Birdie's life to keep their farm. Now that they were doing well, with no huge debts lingering over their heads, they were safe. "Everything's good now. There's no reason to give up."

"It's not giving up," Poopie interjected. "Birdie, the house needs to come down." She stared an earnest hole through Birdie with her big brown eyes.

Birdie gaped at her, her heart thumping sickly, and Poopie clearly had difficulty going on. Walter continued for her.

"I'm getting older, Birdie. You have your own life now." He gestured to the ring Birdie was wearing on her left ring finger. "The idea of having a new house built here . . . it's just more than I can handle. Poopie and I want to enjoy life for a while. We thought we'd move close to where you'll be going to school. You can come home on weekends."

Home. She felt her stomach roll.

She looked to Murphy to plead the case. Murphy had the power to talk anyone into or out of anything. She had once talked the manager of Wendy's into giving her a free milk shake after she had just been caught stealing one of their giant rolls of toilet paper as a joke. But Murphy only looked at her hands thoughtfully.

"Birdie?" Poopie stared at her searchingly.

Birdie cleared her throat. "Can I be excused?"

She got up from the table without waiting for a reply. She walked into her dad's office and closed the door behind her, knowing she was leaving a scene in which she was supposed to be participating like an adult. She leaned against the door, gazing at the piles of paper on the desk, the shelves and shelves of books on insects and fruit bearing and crop yields and business planning, the old photo albums, the books that had been here since before the Darlingtons had even moved in, books that belonged to the house itself. Years of effort, work, and memories were stored up in this room.

Birdie walked to her dad's desk and sank down behind it, staring at his computer. She looked at her left hand and twirled her ring around her finger. She felt like every moment counted. Like she needed to figure out which lifeboat she wanted to be on. She reached for the mouse and pulled up the Internet, then opened her Gmail account.

E,

I'm sorry I didn't show up yesterday. I was confused.

She typed as quickly as she could.

You're going to get a letter in the mail from me. Please throw it away before you read it. I am home in Georgia. I want you to come for the harvest. Please come. I am sorry. And please write back. I love you.

She signed it, *Love, B.* And then she hit Send.

Tap tap tap. Tap tap tap. Thunk! Screech.

"What's she doing?"

Thunk!

Leeda stared at Murphy from across the table and shrugged. And then they both turned as, with a long, scraping noise, Birdie's feet appeared on the stairs, followed by a large cardboard box.

Thunk thunk thunk! Birdie yanked the box down the stairs and, without looking at them or into the kitchen at all, dragged it along the hallway and out the door. This had been going on for about half an hour. Every few minutes Birdie came in or out. On the out, she was always dragging something bizarre behind her— luggage, a two-by-four, blankets. Each time she tromped past them, bumping along, she was trying to pretend they weren't there but clearly wanting them to notice her.

"Maybe she's running away," Murphy said. Leeda just stared blankly at the hallway.

"With all that stuff?" she asked softly.

"Where did she find that two-by-four?" Poopie muttered, more to herself than to anyone sitting at the table. She had her chin resting on her hands, her lips pressed tightly together. She seemed slightly angry, slightly exasperated, and, still, a little wounded.

"It's like she's a ferret," Murphy said.

Leeda stood and walked to the window near the front door. She stared at Birdie, her heart going out to her. Leeda felt like if the orchard went, a part of her would go too. But it would be Birdie's loss more than anyone's. Birdie and the farm were like a single entity. Imagining Birdie without this place was like imagining someone half-complete.

Birdie had dragged her strange collection to the foot of the big oak tree on the right side of the lawn. Apparently two of the items she had retrieved were a hammer and a box of nails.

Suddenly Leeda realized what she was doing. "Oh."

Everyone—Poopie, Walter, and Murphy—came to the window and gawked.

"Is that . . . ?" Murphy said.

"Oh, she is going to fall out, break her neck. Mark this word," said Poopie.

Birdie was starting fresh, away from everyone.

She was building a tree house.

Nine

*P*rimrose Cottage, the home of the late, great Grandmom Eugenie, was just like a dollhouse. It curtsied its way out of its rolling lawn in white frills, decorative latticework, gingerbread window treatments, and romantic slate roof tiles. Eugenie—intrepid, determined, and more than a little spoiled—had hired an architect to build it as an exact replica of a dollhouse she'd had as a girl.

Stepping out of her car, Leeda was surprised to see a tiny Chihuahua tied to the banister of the front porch. Seeing her, he licked his lips excitedly and trembled, stretching out his paws and trying to pull forward. Leeda walked uncertainly up the bottom few stairs, just out of its reach. What was it doing here? It must belong to the guy Eugenie had left in charge of the ponies. Leeda had learned, through talking with her grandmom's lawyer afterward, that he had worked for her grandmom for about a year before she died, though only for a few hours a day. Leeda had never met him. Now he was staying in one of the house's small guest rooms until Leeda could get everything sorted out. But why would he tie his dog to the banister?

Leeda wasn't an animal person. The closest she had ever come to having pets was when she'd hung out with Birdie's dogs, and then she'd accidentally run over one of them. She had ridden one of Grandmom Eugenie's ponies at her seventh birthday party, but it had eaten the pink ribbon from her dress and had died of an intestinal blockage. Maybe it was her track record as the Angel of Death to God's four-legged friends, but for whatever reason, she didn't feel comfortable around them. They liked to put their tongues on your face. Sometimes they wanted you to scratch right above their butts. They had no sense of boundaries. Leave it to her muleheaded grandmom to force her desires on Leeda despite Leeda's obvious inclinations to the contrary.

Thinking the caretaker was most likely out back, Leeda turned away from the stairs and walked over to the side of the house, turning the corner to where the grass was shaded from the morning sun. Bees were buzzing over the tiny white flowers that grew up the fence posts of the pony corral. Beyond, she could see a figure in the barn lot, standing in a filmy cloud of flying pony fur, dust, and a knot of gnats. He moved rigidly, stiffly. He looked up and noticed her. She plucked at the peeling paint on the gate while she waited for him to come over.

As he got closer, her smile faltered a bit, and she felt a lop-sided rhythm in her wrists. He was younger than he'd seemed from far away—a lot closer to her age. He wasn't handsome, per se. But there was something about the way he looked that made her feel a little wobbly. He had shaggy brown hair and blue eyes overhung by straight, dark eyebrows. His face was angular, his nose broad and straight. His movements were angular too. But there was something vital about the way he moved.

She stuck out her hand, overcompensating for her sudden wobbliness by speaking in a voice that was all business. "Hi, I'm Leeda. You must be Grey Backe."

He took her hand, expressionless. "How's it going?"

"You're the caretaker, I take it. Very nice to meet you." She knew she sounded like her mother, all formal and polite, but she couldn't help it.

"Yeah." He gave her a once-over, taking in her black rubber boots with the buckles, her white leggings, and the clipboard tucked neatly under her arm. Leeda realized self-consciously that maybe she had overdressed, and she fidgeted in her boots.

With a stiff, reluctant movement, Grey propelled himself toward the maroon metal gate and began fiddling with the latch, opening it with a creak and indicating that she should enter. About twenty feet away, a knot of ponies watched them curiously.

"Thanks," Leeda said, stepping in and watching around her feet. It must have rained recently, because the ground was soggy and littered with small puddles that threatened to sully her boots. Sullying was something Leeda was used to from the orchard, but she always avoided it when she could.

Grey closed the gate behind her, sliding the metal Y of the latch back around the post of the door. Leeda turned on a charming smile for him, but he didn't look at her. He walked toward the stables, across the muddy field. Leeda, unsure whether she was supposed to follow or not, started after him.

The stable consisted of a long, wide rectangle, open to the air but for an overhanging roof perched on posts. On each side of a long middle hallway were wooden pens—about fifteen to a side. Grey wove to the left instead of going on and led Leeda to the back, where a sort of wooden shed was attached.

"Tack room's in here," he said, opening the door and showing her into a dirt-floored room full of saddles, buckets, ropes, halters, and instruments of all sorts—brushes and weird silver-tipped things Leeda didn't recognize. It smelled like leather and oil and old hay, pleasant and earthy. On the opposite wall was another door, and Grey led her through that to the long row of stalls.

"You put them in here every day?" Leeda asked, realizing Grey wasn't going to offer the information.

"Only when it's really cold, or in bad weather, or for grooming and feeding." The stalls were small—the doors were only a little higher than Leeda's waist. The stable looked more like somewhere the seven dwarves would live than a place that housed actual creatures. And, appropriately, each stall had a sign hanging from its swinging wooden door: *Mitzie, Tinkles, Sleepy, Sneezy, Chauncy, The Baron, Mr. Jinxy.*

Grey's hand moved along the top of the doors as he walked. He stopped to do tiny things here and there—move a shovel to its rightful place, tie up a rope—his dirty hands moving like afterthoughts. Leeda got the feeling, even through the tiny movements, that he was strong and quick. He didn't look back at her once.

They came out at the end and stepped off the concrete platform into the dirt, back into view of the ponies, who had gathered in the early morning shade of some trees that hung over the fence. They were comical to look at, like cartoon characters, squat and a little rounded at the belly. There were a few speckled ones, but most of them were solid colors—dark brown, tan, or black, with patches of white here and there.

They peered back at Leeda as she eyed them warily. A few were nibbling at leaves. Some gathered in little groups. The rest stood in a sociable knot, as if they were all gossiping about something, casting Leeda glances as if she were the one being gossiped about.

"Oh." Leeda suddenly remembered. "Is that your Chihuahua on the porch?"

Grey shook his head. "People assume because we're a pony rescue, we're also an animal rescue. You'll need to let me know what you want me to do with all the strays that show up."

"What did Grandm—what did Eugenie have you do?"

"The pound," Grey said.

Leeda cringed. "That's terrible." The pound was at the edge of town toward the highway. Birdie never let Leeda drive past it when she was in the car. It made her too sad that they put animals to sleep.

"Do you want to keep them instead?" he asked, looking at her directly. Leeda could tell it was a kind of challenge. He expected her to say no, of course.

"Um, I'll have to get back to you," she said. "You can just . . . feed him till then, and whatever else."

Grey nodded, and they stood in silence, watching the ponies hoof about the lot. "Do you want me to show you how to halter them?" Grey asked, sounding put out. "So you can bring them in yourself when you need to?"

"Oh." Leeda looked at the ponies. "Oh, God, no." She cleared her throat. "I don't really like animals."

"Too messy," Grey said evenly, taking in her outfit again. His tone wasn't kind.

Leeda stiffened. The guy clearly didn't like her off the bat. She decided she didn't like him back. She straightened her spine.

"Too demanding," she said, flicking a blond tendril back coolly. "Anyway, I need their names so I can list them online," she said. "I think people like to know names. Better marketing."

Grey studied her critically for a moment. "Those are Sneezy and The Baron," he said, pointing to two that were off on their own, huddled together front to back, so their tails were swishing at each other's chests. "They're helping each other with flies. The other ponies don't like Sneezy, but The Baron stands up for her. They're pals." He pointed to the darkest one, then along to the others. "Mitzie is the beauty. Sleepy is sleepy all the time. Tinkles is clueless and she eats leaves even though they make her puke. Just in case you can use any of that for marketing."

Leeda arched an eyebrow at him, realizing she was probably being mocked. Her grandmom had started "rescuing" them when Leeda was a toddler, though Leeda and her sister had always considered it more as "collecting." She had seen them on a pretty regular basis all her life; she'd never thought of them as having alliances, enmities, and weird little quirks.

Grey started leading her back toward the gate.

"Did you go to Bridgewater High School?" she asked.

Grey shook his head. Leeda waited for him to offer where he had gone to school, but he didn't.

"I'm probably going to get an MBA. I'm at Columbia," she offered, just to keep the conversation going without feeling so awkward, and to let him know she was not mockery material. "I want to go into marketing."

Grey leaned on the fence once they got there, turned around, and looked at her. "Your grandmom treated the ponies like people," he said.

"I know," Leeda admitted. Grandmom Eugenie hadn't just loved the ponies—they'd been her life. She used to have birthday parties for them. She'd loved to talk about them on the phone and had sometimes made Leeda talk to them on the cordless.

"For some people it's easier to love animals than people," Grey said diffidently. "I wonder why a lot of people who have everything tend to be out of touch with their hearts. Like their soul's cut off below the neck or something."

Leeda could feel her face flushing. She didn't know exactly where, but she knew some line was being crossed, and she felt invaded. What he was saying about Eugenie was close to things she'd thought herself from time to time.

"Look, Grey, I don't know what I expected when I got here, but it wasn't someone being insensitive about my grandmother, who's dead. So please just stick to your job." She stared at him for a minute, then couldn't help adding, "I already know the people in my family."

Grey calmly stuck his hands in his pockets, studying her, irritatingly unfazed. Leeda wondered if she'd gone too far, but at the moment, she didn't care.

"I should just let you know that I'm leaving in early August," he said. "I'll be here till then to get you situated and all. After that, you'll be on your own with the ponies."

It was Leeda's turn to be unruffled. "My plan is to move them pretty fast. I shouldn't need you more than a couple of weeks at the most." On her way here, she had worried about telling him this because she knew she was taking work away from him. But now, it felt satisfying.

Grey laughed.

Leeda brushed her hair from her eyes, annoyed. "What?"

"You'll be lucky if you can get rid of them by the end of the summer." He grinned as if he were about to reveal something shocking. And then, he did. "Your grandmom was trying to find homes for them for years."

Leeda ignored the Chihuahua, who was straining at her and whining, as she passed him on her way into the house. She closed the door with a creak and stared into the dimness.

Eugenie's front parlor had always been like a room in a museum—clean, orderly, and perfect. Leeda had once, as a kid, spilled a pitcher of sweet tea on the couch, and she had thought her grandmom was going to keel over from the shock of it. True to her southern roots, she had literally swooned. But now that Eugenie was gone, the room felt even more stifling than it had before. There were two uncomfortable brocade couches, a piano against the far wall, two tiny side tables, and a large buffet pinning down the room, covered in white doilies that were slowly turning yellow. Everything was coated in a fine layer of dust.

Leeda was reminded of long afternoons she'd spent with her grandmother here—sometimes on a visit with her mom and sometimes when her mom had sent her alone. It had always felt like there was an absence of air. But Eugenie had seemed to like it that way.

Now Leeda opened the curtains, sending a cloud of dust flying around her, and glanced out the window toward the barn lot where Grey was pouring a huge bucket of water into one of the troughs. At least he was strong. Leeda couldn't see pouring bucketfuls of water with her spindly little arms.

With a sudden urge to call Eric, she went into the green linoleum–floored kitchen and picked up the phone, placing it to her ear, but there was no dial tone. She sighed, frustrated. She probably would have to get the line reconnected. What if it was as hard to get rid of the ponies as Grey had said? What if she ended up stuck at Primrose Cottage all summer? She walked back out of the kitchen again and up the carpeted stairs to her grandmom's bedroom, where Eugenie had always kept an olive green rotary phone. Maybe it was working.

Leeda pushed the bedroom door open and tiptoed across the carpet as if she might wake someone. She picked up the phone on the bedside table but it too was dead. Leeda sank onto the bed with a creak and looked around the room, pointlessly annoyed at her grandmom. The room still smelled like her powdery perfume. Her clothes still hung in the closet, the door of which stood open. It was as though she had just stepped out for the afternoon.

An old pocket calendar from 1984 sat on the nightstand. Leeda stared at it for a moment and then, acting on impulse, she tucked it into her purse. She had done something similar at the orchard the other day while Birdie was building her tree house. She'd found a half of a crayon tucked into the corner of the living room, and had pocketed it when no one was looking. She didn't know why she'd done it. But, she reasoned, she wasn't hurting anyone.

Leeda swung her legs against the bed frame, but something pricked her right in her calf. She bent to see what it was, lifting up the thin white bed skirt. It was an envelope, maybe a letter. *Probably from President Reagan,* Leeda thought drily. She tugged it out of its spot and studied it.

It was yellowed, and it had no address or postmark, only Eugenie's name. On the back, where the seal met in a triangle, someone had drawn a little heart. It was a love letter.

Leeda felt a prick of tenderness and sadness that her grandmom was gone, her annoyance evaporating.

Leeda considered a moment, feeling guilty. And then she opened it. The date was written in a sloppy hand—May 31, 1937. The date had significance to Leeda. Her mother had a plate on the wall commemorating her parents' wedding date above one commemorating her own marriage. This letter had been written a couple of weeks before Eugenie's wedding.

> *Genie,*
>
> *You've really outdone yourself this time.*
>
> *Edgar will be fine, though the doctor was worried at first that he had a concussion. Who would have thought a flying hymnal could knock a boy down like that? I know you don't like "Hosanna in the Highest," but at least you could keep yourself from flinging the words into the choir.*
>
> *Emmaline at the Pop 'N' Shop says that you're a menace. She says you're like a rubber band, constantly propelling your body this way and that. I stood up for you and told her that her body was like a zucchini squash. I said you couldn't help it if you're more alive than she is.*

When you were getting the talk from the reverend after church today, you looked so sorry and so defiant at the same time, and I just wanted to kiss you. But I'll wait for the moonlight under the trees for that.

The trees are beautiful. You are beautiful. I'll see you tonight.

Leeda smiled gently. Leeda's grandfather had died when she was a little kid. She had never thought of him and her grandmom as being in love. She had never imagined anyone, even her grandfather, as being so free and informal with the formidable Eugenie. Eugenie had been the kind of person you didn't feel comfortable discussing anything deeper with than the state of the weather and how you were doing in school. But here Leeda's grandfather was, pouring out intimate observations.

Finally Leeda's eyes reached the bottom of the page. Her heart skipped a beat. She pulled the letter to her chest, irrationally, and looked out the window, as if someone might be looking in, spying. She held the letter out in front of her again, as if it might sort itself back into what she'd expected, even taken for granted. She checked the date again—it had been written right before her grandparents' wedding.

And there, at the bottom of the page, signed next to a tiny heart, was a simple letter *M*.

Leeda's grandfather's name was Frank.

Ten

Murphy sat cross-legged on the floor of the women's dorm, pulling her nubby red sweatshirt over her bent knees. She stuffed her hands into her suitcase and pulled out a stack of T-shirts, flinging them onto the bed. Already the room looked like it had been hit by a tornado, even though everything had come out of her tiny suitcase.

Murphy's mom, hurt at first when Murphy had announced her plans, had eventually agreed to let Murphy move into the orchard dorms as long as they hung out on the weekends and had dinner during the week as often as she could. The truth was that they both knew living at the orchard would keep Murphy occupied and happy—instead of restless and bored. When Murphy got restless and bored, she got creative and a little deviant.

Once the workers arrived—only a week away—the nights would be full of chatter and laughter and stories and card games. And even now, when it was empty, the dorm house—situated as it was in the middle of nature—was exciting and different. The dorms had been built just that year. The paint smelled fresh.

The floors smelled like plywood. But the view out the window by her bed was the same as it had been: some scrubby gatherings of trees, the trail to the garden, and the occasional bird, hunting worms and bugs in the grass.

Finished packing, she hopped up and bounced a little on her heels, wondering what to get into. Poopie and Walter had gone into town for food supplies. No doubt they'd return with body-sized sacks of rice and beans and gallons of orange juice. Birdie had retreated to her tree house and was hammering away, unwilling to come down.

Birdie had been mum about what had happened in Mexico, though. Murphy knew it had to have something to do with Enrico. When she asked Birdie if they'd broken the engagement, she had only said, "Not really," and had asked if they could talk about something else. Poopie had been beside herself about Birdie living in a tree, and she could often be seen standing at the bottom of the ladder, holding some food she'd made. Murphy assumed Birdie hadn't opened up to Poopie either. But she knew that would have to happen in time.

Murphy walked down the hallway and out onto the grass, deciding to head to the house and use the computer. She could e-mail some friends, order some new sneakers. She trudged across the grass, waving to Birdie on the way, and walked inside. The house was muffled and silent. Murphy walked into Walter's office, the walls paneled in wood, the floor covered in an old, thick rug. She sat on the chair in front of the desk with a creak and powered up the computer, then logged into her Yahoo! account. She had a bunch of e-mails from New York, a couple of them from guys, which she ignored.

When she'd read them all, her hand hovered over the mouse for a minute and then moved, maybe as she had been planning all along, to the *Blah Blah Blah* folder.

She opened the first e-mail.

You won't believe it, Shorts, but Bridgewater misses you. The lady at Dunkin' Donuts asked about you the other morning at the drive-through. And Mrs. Hobbes at my dad's store said she misses your "high spirits." I think that's a euphemism for delinquent behavior. The point being, I'm not the only one who thinks about you here. But I may be the only one who thinks about you last thing before I go to sleep.

So how's New York? What have you done so far? Have you seen anyone famous? Does it make you feel big? Small?

Drop your small-town ex a line and let me know how well you've moved on. I won't hold it against you. Back here in Bridgewater, there's some giant black hole on my porch where you used to be. But I'm happy for you, Shorts. I'm just happy.

R.

The e-mails were all similar. Simple and sweet and undemanding. She read them in order. Rex asked a bunch of questions about what she was doing, what her classes were, what things she loved most about the city. He told her small snippets of his life—that he had gotten really into building furniture;

occasionally he mentioned his dad and how he sometimes asked about her. Murphy felt a pang now that she couldn't understand. Nowhere did Rex mention leaving Bridgewater or anything that might draw him and his dad away.

Finally she was at the last e-mail, the arrow hovering over the icon. She let out a small sigh and let her finger click it, like it was the last part of a conversation she didn't want to end.

Murphy,

This is my last message. I wonder if you've read any of them. I wouldn't put it past you not to. You're a little messed up like that. But I don't feel like I've wasted my time.

I like to picture you in New York. I like to think you found everything you wanted. I like to think of you laughing a lot with all these people you meet. Maybe even with another guy. It doesn't matter about the other guy, if he exists. I want happiness for you.

I can't stop picturing your face. Picturing it when you're looking at paintings at all the museums. Picture it after a long day of studying. Picturing it when you and Leeda are cracking up about something. It makes it impossible to be mad at you. It makes me happy that you're free, like you always said you wanted.

I guess maybe I'll see you when you get home. But I think we'll both be different. I think I will have let you go. I think you will have done the same. I just hope that we don't feel like strangers. I don't ever want to feel like I don't know you.

See you, maybe.
R.

Murphy stared at the e-mail. She read it twice more, wanting to hold on to it, not wanting it to be something from a time that was gone. She heaved a deep, shuddering sigh.

"This is stupid," she whispered to herself. She lowered her head against the keyboard until it started beeping. She shut the computer down and stood up, her legs tingling and asleep, the pang inside deeper and bigger and indescribable.

She walked out onto the porch of the house and leaned on the railing. She looked toward the tree house, a big wooden box in the branches made of plywood and cloth like a little nest. The sound of Birdie's hammer echoed across the grass.

Murphy slid indecisively down the stairs, stared at her bike where it lay on the grass that met the gravel drive, and finally climbed on and pedaled out onto Orchard Road.

All she could think was that she had been betrayed. The thing she remembered most about all of the e-mails was that Rex hadn't said good-bye.

The trailer glittered dully in the afternoon light. She could hear her mom in the shower. Jodee always liked to rinse off after a day at the office.

Murphy poured herself a Mountain Dew from the fridge

and stared around listlessly, then began rifling through the mail sitting on the counter, looking for something shallow and absorbing—a *People*, an *Entertainment Weekly*—to take away the needy feeling she had inside. She flipped through a Victoria's Secret catalog. Then she moved on to the pile of older papers lodged between the ceramic cookie jar and the George Foreman grill.

The papers in the pile were mostly bills, with the occasional late payment notice, and flyers for local business openings that Jodee hadn't bothered to throw away. Murphy breezed past an envelope and then, curious, came back to it.

It was from Dooly County Memorial Hospital, and it had her name on it. It was addressed to her mother, but the line beneath that read *Re: Murphy Ann McGowen*. It was also paper-clipped to another letter.

Murphy opened the envelope and unfolded its contents, scanning them.

The allele sizes of the different DNA markers examined and used in the statistical analysis portion of the test . . .

It was all Greek to her. Had her mom had Murphy's hair tested for some horrible disease? Murphy tried to picture her mom stealing hair off her brush like a witch doctor.

She unclipped the attached paper and read that. It said something about legal proceedings, a date—June tenth at 3 p.m.—and a meeting with Judge Abbott at the Bridgewater Courthouse.

She turned back to the hospital notice, a possibility taking shape in her mind, her heart pounding as she read more thoroughly. There were index values. A 99.99 percent probability. She felt a wave of nausea. The paper began to tremble, and Murphy realized her hand was shaking.

And then there was a step behind her, and the pile was being snatched out of her grip.

"That's my mail!" Jodee said, standing behind her with her hair half dry. Murphy turned to face her.

"Mom—"

"Didn't anyone ever tell you to respect other people's privacy?" Jodee was making a show of only being peeved as she tucked the papers under her arm. But her lips, pulled tightly together, trembled.

"Mom, what's that paper?"

"Nothing. I'm going to be late; I made plans for dinner tonight," Jodee said, turning on her heel and heading back to the bathroom, where she checked herself in the mirror, or at least pretended to. She grabbed her purse. The papers remained firmly lodged under her armpit.

"Mom—"

"Murphy, it's my mail and none of your business."

Before Murphy could do anything, Jodee was outside.

"Mom!" Murphy flung the door open to follow her, feeling desperate, like something huge and important was slipping out of her fingers.

"Mom, that's a paternity test, isn't it?"

Murphy's head was spinning. She felt too small for the throbbing in her gut.

"Mom . . . ?"

Jodee slammed the door of the Pontiac and started the engine. Murphy yelled after her even though the windows were up, the engine was blasting, and there was no way she could hear. "Mom, does this mean you found my dad?!"

The tires peeled in the driveway, and Jodee was gone.

Judge Miller Abbott had not been an adventurous teenager. He always stayed after school to help clean the erasers. He was a member of the Bridgewater High School Debate Team, the Dooly County Dapper Dans, and the Young Republicans. He met his wife at a cotillion. For weeks after his wedding, he woke feeling like he was forgetting something, like maybe he'd forgotten to pay the caterer or had a library book that he hadn't returned. For some reason this feeling was always accompanied by a desire to drive to the orchard and howl at the moon.

Eleven

*B*irdie and Leeda sat at the decrepit picnic table behind the women's dorm, kicking each other's feet under the table and picking at the peeling wood. Murphy stood over the outdoor sink, running her hair and the back of her neck under the faucet. Majestic pounced around the yard a few feet away, chasing a bee.

Leeda was on her BlackBerry, looking like she was about to spontaneously combust. Birdie was thinking about the lostness that had snagged inside her. There was no other way to describe it. She had felt it since the day she had come home and gotten the news about the farm from her dad and Poopie. Maybe she had even felt it before that. Maybe it had been the lostness that had caused Birdie to send the letter about Enrico's pants.

"What? No, I need to leave the return flight open-ended." Leeda tapped Birdie's feet with her own. She pulled the phone away from her ear to stare down at the screen, and then put it back to her cheek and mouthed to Birdie, *The reception sucks.*

It was midday and they'd been working hard all morning, snapping the linens onto the beds in the dorms, mopping the floors and scrubbing the cobwebs out of the sinks, dragging the harvesting harnesses out to where they'd be ready to use first thing tomorrow. The workers would be arriving anytime this afternoon. What Birdie hadn't counted on was being ready for them and having nothing more to do but wait.

Cynthia Darlington had brought lunch from the teahouse—finger sandwiches, iced mint tea, macaroni salad—stayed for half an hour, and rushed back to work. They had chatted about the teahouse, about people in town, and about Walter's and Poopie's plans to move.

Birdie could tell she'd wanted to ask about Enrico too, but didn't force the issue out of respect for Birdie's privacy.

She kept thinking about what her dad had said when he and Poopie told her about the orchard. That she had her own life now. It had sounded like he and Poopie felt they'd been set free. If they did feel that way, Birdie knew they deserved it. But it made Birdie's heart ache. Because she didn't feel she had her own life at all.

"Okay, June tenth, that's fine." Leeda rolled her eyes at Birdie. "Uh huh. Yes."

The days leading up to the harvest had always been agonizing for Birdie. As a kid, it had meant waiting for Luis to give her piggyback rides so she was towering over the peach trees, or for Emma to sit gently beside her to show her needlepoint, or for Raeka to prop her up on the counter to watch while she boiled a bag full of black beans and got them ready to sauté. Because she was homeschooled, Birdie had always treasured the orchard filled with familiar friends. Waiting for summer was a lot like waiting for Santa Claus to come. Then, as she'd gotten older, the feeling had turned to one of restlessness for activity and action, waiting for the chance to socialize and to wear her impatient body out with physical labor. But this year, she was like an inhaled breath. She had hung herself up on a question. Would he come? Wouldn't he? The wondering was almost a welcome distraction from thinking about other woulds and wouldn'ts. Like, what would her house sound like if they tore it down?

Leeda finally got off the phone, shaking her head. "I'm never gonna get out of here," she said.

"What's the rush?" Murphy gurgled.

"No rush," Leeda said, looking unsure. "Just . . . I told Eric I'd be back. I miss him."

"Aww." Murphy pulled back from the sink to make little kissy faces. Leeda stuck out her tongue at her.

"There are all these great things we're supposed to do," Leeda said, defending herself as she took a sip of her lemonade. She looked funny, sweaty and red-faced, a cobweb stuck in her hair, holding her BlackBerry and sitting with perfect posture. Murphy pulled away from the sink completely, her hair dripping down her forest green tank top, and mumbled, "Your turn."

Birdie and Leeda took turns dunking themselves under the icy cold sink water. With water dripping off her nose and gathering at her lips, Leeda looked like a forties pinup girl. Birdie pulled her own hair from where it stuck to her face. She probably looked like bigfoot.

"Let's get in the shade," Murphy said, flopping her head across the picnic table as if across a soft mattress. A june bug landed on one of her curls, and then lit off again.

Birdie picked up Majestic, tucking her under her arm, and led them out of the shade onto the lawn and across the grass to her tree house.

They climbed the ladder, cresting the landing and settling down onto the plywood floor and across the mattress Birdie had managed to haul up. Majestic lay down at Birdie's feet, her butterfly-like ears swiveling and twitching like satellites.

In the two weeks since Birdie had started building it, the tree house had started to feel like home. At the top of her bed, which was just a twin mattress from her room, stood her little wooden bookcase filled with favorite books: *501 Spanish Verbs, Birds of South America, The Book of Tarot,* and her collection of World Book Encyclopedias. On top of the shelf, she had put a little vase full of survivor flowers from Murphy's decrepit garden. Because it was nestled in the leaf-thickened limbs, it was gloriously cool and shady. The sweat was drying so quickly on Birdie's body that she was suddenly chilly. She ran her fingers through her long hair, reddish in the light coming through the leaves, and started to braid it.

Murphy lay back, making herself at home, and propped her feet up against the trunk of the tree. Up here, the orchard took on an orderly, geometric look. It fell into a pattern that couldn't be seen from the ground for all the chaos of leaves and colors and bugs and birds. Birdie, unable to sleep for the last few nights, liked to sit up in the dark, stretched out under the moon, and watch and listen to it all. She would swear she could almost hear the tree itself growing.

"Well, I should have known your grandmom was a ho." Murphy's arms lolled to her sides as her feet stuck up in the air. Leeda had told them about the mysterious letter she had found in her grandmom's room.

"Hey, take it easy on the tree," Birdie said, staring at where Murphy was chipping away at the bark with her heels.

Murphy looked down at her feet, and then laid them flat on the wooden floor.

"I wonder why she married my grandfather," Leeda mused, "if she and this guy were so in love."

"I wonder who he was," Birdie said.

"I wonder who my dad is," Murphy interjected, trying to sound jovial.

Leeda studied Murphy. "Are you gonna try to talk to your mom again?"

Murphy put her feet back up on the tree, absently digging off the bark again.

"She won't admit it."

"How can she not admit something you actually saw?" Leeda asked.

Murphy's face looked bored. Only her violent, destructive feet showed any anger. "My mom is the queen of denial. One time, she was laying on the horn because the car in front of us was letting someone out on the sidewalk, and when I told her that was obnoxious, she said she wasn't doing anything. I said, 'Mom, you're laying on the horn.' And she said, 'No I'm not.' That's how my mom feels about denial. It's just something you do even when you know no one believes you." Murphy blinked up at the sky. "Whatever. I don't care in this huge way. I mean, I want to know. I'm mad at her and everything. But I'm not like, 'I miss my absentee dad,' or anything. I've never thought about him all that much."

She sat up and perused the items on Birdie's shelves, clearly wanting to get off the subject. Birdie's eyes trailed to the driveway, magnetized, as they had been doing all day.

"Birdie, why do you have Nicorette?" Murphy was looking at Birdie's shelf. Sure enough, a pack of Nicorette gum was sitting on the middle shelf.

Birdie felt herself blushing. "I'm taking up smoking."

The way Murphy looked at Birdie, tucking her chin and looking up from under her eyebrows, made Leeda laugh. It lightened the mood.

"If you want to take up smoking, which is idiotic, why are you chewing gum instead of actually, um, smoking?" Murphy pressed.

"I hate the taste of cigarettes." Birdie had just thought smoking would be a good, cynical thing to do, given the circumstances.

Murphy blinked at her for a moment, and then relaxed, laying her head back down. "I bet my dad smokes."

Birdie stared at Murphy thoughtfully. They lapsed into silence. Birdie could hear the creaking of the pecan trees over beyond the dorms carried on the breeze. She twirled her ring nervously, like it was a kind of rosary.

A car came and went down Orchard Drive, the hum of the motor faint in the distance. Majestic's satellite ears followed it down the road.

Birdie had the feeling of teetering on a wire.

The sound of another vehicle echoed faintly across the grass. As it got closer, it wheezed. It could be a truck carrying rocks or lumber. But as it got louder, it squeaked and wheezed again, distinctly buslike. Murphy, Leeda, and Birdie looked at each other. Birdie's heart fluttered up to her throat. Then Murphy bounced up and grinned at them, turning to slither down the ladder. Leeda followed her. Birdie grabbed Majestic and trailed Leeda, her hands unsteady on the rungs.

The bus chugged its way up the driveway, hands squiggling out of it to wave like the legs of a caterpillar. At the top of the driveway, it slowed with a squeal, let out a gasp of air, and stopped. A moment later, the doors came open with a hiss.

Out poured some of Birdie's oldest friends. Birdie let herself be swept into the group for hugs and kisses and pats on the back. She made her way through the crowd, searching the faces, looking for the one who would save her from whatever the lostness was.

When the last passenger had emerged and they were all moving forward to meet the crowd, Birdie kept her smile big. She climbed up the bus stairs, like she was making sure no one had left anything behind, and scanned the empty aisle, the empty seats, the places where he wasn't.

Contrary to popular belief, Poopie Pedraza of Darlington Orchard had not seen the Virgin Mary in the clouds once, but twice. The first time had been the day she'd arrived in Bridgewater. The second was the day that she'd met her employer's niece, little Leeda Cawley-Smith, out in the front lawn, where she stood, three years old, tweeting at the birds. Poopie saw the cloud just then, directly overhead, and decided that this child was most likely destined to become a nun. She crossed herself and went back inside.

Twelve

Leeda woke in her dorm room in a bed across from Murphy's. She'd been having a dream about Eric. Nothing exciting. Just being in a cab with him, talking for some reason about the bees at the orchard.

Now she blinked, studying the bare white walls, slowly focusing and looking at the floor where Murphy's things had snaked their way across the room, claiming the entire width of it. She listened to the quietness in the building and out beyond the window, relishing the stillness until she heard someone open one of the doors across the hall.

As it had the summer before, getting up over the past few mornings had taken on a snowball effect. Whoever was up first, no matter how quiet they were, woke the others, and everyone started to get up and prepare themselves for a long day of work. Leeda slid out of bed, wide awake, and nudged Murphy to wake her. "Pickin' time," she whispered. Murphy growled at her before Leeda walked out into the hall.

In the kitchen, the women were eating quick bowls of cereal and oatmeal before heading out to the fields to pick. It had only taken a few days for the orchard work to fall into a pattern. Up at dawn, quick breakfast, and out to pick in the morning air before the sun got too hot. Then quit at midday to wolf down food and rest for an hour, usually in the shade of the common room, which wasn't air-conditioned but was still many degrees cooler than outside. And then back to pick for the afternoon.

Last night, before she'd fallen into bed exhausted, after a luke-warm shower to wash away the peach juice, Leeda had promised herself that this morning she'd go back to Primrose Cottage and check on the ponies. But now that she was up, she knew that, as on the previous days, she wouldn't do it. She'd spent a couple of after-noons on Uncle Walter's computer, doing Internet searches on var-ious pony, horse, and animal rescues and calling any that looked promising. But going back and dealing with Grey and the gaggle of little souls in the corral had been too unappealing.

So instead, when they were all done with breakfast, Leeda fol-lowed the others out into the fields. She and Murphy moved a few feet apart, their backs turned to each other, taking different sides of the same row.

They were picking June Princes, which grew in an area of trees up toward the front of the house. Behind her, Murphy, sweaty and flushed, swatted at the branches with a vengeance, knocking the peaches into the canvas harness attached across her chest and stomach. There was no use telling her she was going to bruise the peaches. Murphy didn't know how to do things gently. Her hair was standing up halfway and lopsided, and her eyes were bleary. Murphy was no morning person, but she'd also been in a dark mood since the day she'd found the letter at her mom's. She just didn't like to admit it.

Leeda moved down the row slowly, picking expertly, doing a touch test on the fruits whose ripeness she doubted. If she picked them too soon, they wouldn't taste sweet enough because they wouldn't have time to draw in enough sugar. If she picked them too late, she knew, they would have already started producing ethylene, a chemical that ripened them, and they'd be overripe by the time they were sold. Their first summer on the orchard, Birdie had revealed to them that the world of peaches was more intricate and varied than they ever imagined. Clingstones, the ones that clung to their pits, ripened earliest, then semi-frees, and then freestones. Each variety was like a different dog breed with vastly different characteristics—the texture of the meat, the fuzziness of the skin, the strength and sweetness of the flavor.

They worked in silence, and the rustle of the leaves became hypnotic. There was the occasional flash of a white shirt or blue jeans or tan arms moving in the rows up ahead. Someone had started a fire in the eating area between the two gleaming white buildings, getting ready for lunch, and the smell of smoke and something peppery and thick drifted through the air.

Despite her restlessness to get back to New York, Leeda was content and happy, strength flowing through her body. Her muscles ached, but she already felt her limbs growing stronger, her body getting more fluid and muscular at the same time. The fresh air, which smelled amazing compared to the air of the city, was as refreshing as water to her; she took it in with big gulps. She felt calm and centered in a way that New York didn't really allow.

"You know, it's crazy about miniature ponies," Leeda said. "What I was reading on the Internet. People keep them for events, like parties, and then when they get old they just put them to sleep. And they breed these dwarves, only that kind of breeding is really bad for them, and they end up with health problems and things like that."

"I thought you didn't like ponies," Murphy said.

Leeda shrugged, squeezing a peach gently to test it. She plucked it off the branch with a snap.

"I know *I* don't like ponies," Murphy muttered, more to herself than to Leeda. "I don't know why people are so into miniature stuff. Dollhouses, croissants, ponies." She shook her head at the tree in front of her. "So dumb." She looked up at Leeda again, as if she'd just remembered she was there.

"I think I'm gonna take a couple of them to the fair. Kind of like a commercial for miniature ponies. Get the word out."

"You should go over there too. Check on them."

"Bleh," Leeda replied.

"What's the big deal?"

Leeda frowned. "The ponies just stare at me. Like they know about that time the one pony ate my ribbon and died. I think they hate me."

"I don't think ponies know how to hate," Murphy offered ironically. "Especially miniature ponies. I think miniature ponies only think about rainbows."

Leeda felt the weight of her basket with her hands and gave Murphy a look.

Murphy shrugged. "Okay, kidding aside. You can't be good at everything." She turned back to her tree, absently.

Leeda stared at her for a moment, confused about what she'd meant.

Murphy looked at her, noticing. "I mean, you like to be great at things, Lee. At everything. Maybe you're scared you're not good at ponies. Animals are too messy and unpredictable or something. It's not like econ."

"I know I'm not good at ponies," Leeda said.

"Well, you don't *have* to be good at it. You just have to be okay at it until you find a spot for them."

Leeda blinked at Murphy, taking it in. Then she turned and walked up the row to the sorting shed. Birdie and Poopie were sitting there under an overhang in the shade, sorting the peaches into batches to sell locally, to ship, and—if they were mushy or damaged—to turn into cider. The two women looked nothing alike: Poopie—short, thin, and almond-skinned; Birdie—tall, fleshy, with skin like peaches and cream. But they moved with the same mannerisms, developed over years of skilled work, and the same sure hands. A few of the other workers were standing there, gently dumping the contents of their baskets onto the large table. They all stood, wiping sweat off their foreheads and nodding at each other, too tired to talk. Leeda dumped her peaches and then turned back down the row.

Halfway down, the sound of an engine drifted over to her, a car coming up the drive about forty yards away and out of sight. Leeda stopped at her next tree and leaned on one hip, pausing with a ripe peach in her hand, working the soft, mottled fuzz with her fingers, wondering who it was. She saw a sliver of a person crossing the grass toward the sorting shed. "No," she said under her breath.

A moment later, Birdie was happily leading Grey down the row toward where she and Murphy stood. Majestic was nipping along at their heels.

"Hey," Grey said, neither frowning nor smiling at her, just meeting her eyes in a direct blue gaze. He was holding the Chihuahua in his arms, a leash attached to its collar and balled up in his hands.

"Hi," Leeda said, reluctantly polite. "Um, Murphy, this is Grey. Grey, Murphy."

"The guy from the pony corral?" Murphy asked, letting her harness full of peaches dangle like a baby off her hips.

Leeda sighed an assent and looked to the ground at the peaches rotting there. She stepped on a dry leaf to make a crunching sound.

"I was wondering what you want me to do with this dog," Grey said. "You haven't been to the house, so . . ." Leeda looked down at the animal. He was still trembling, whether out of fear or excitement it was hard to tell. It looked, more than anything, like a trembling of longing. Like the dog was in a constant state of wanting something he didn't have. He shot the same needy look at Leeda, Birdie, and Murphy, and then dolefully back at Grey.

Leeda was mesmerized by his wild, rampant insecurity. It made her feel heavy inside.

"Bird, do you want a dog?" she asked, suddenly hopeful.

Birdie, her long auburn hair all tangled and messy from sleeping in a tree, her cheeks rosy, had a picnic basket dangling from her elbow. Suddenly on the spot, she stared at the dog, her eyes dark and huge and sympathetic but dubious. "I don't think Dad wants another dog."

Leeda gave the Chihuahua one more glance and sighed. "I guess you just need to take him . . ." She looked sideways at Birdie, and then looked at Grey meaningfully. ". . . to those people. The ones you took them to when Grandmom was around?"

Grey looked between her and Birdie, confused for a second, and then—mercifully—just nodded. "Okay."

"Do you want to come to our picnic?" Birdie chirped. Leeda gave her a death look, but Birdie remained oblivious to it.

Murphy turned and swiped away at the nearest tree as if she hadn't heard.

"You're killing the peaches," Birdie said forlornly, staring into Murphy's basket. Murphy looked too, guilty. Birdie tugged Grey by the sleeve and pulled him good-naturedly along with her.

Grey looked at Leeda questioningly. Leeda squinted back at him and followed the group into the trees.

They walked straight down one of the rows, heading deep enough in that they could see nothing but peach trees in any direction. Up ahead, Murphy swerved left into a stand of taller, older trees. These weren't harvested anymore and grew wild and unwieldy. They held the occasional gnarled peach but nothing more. The dense rows gave way to a thin patch of woods that hung overhead, dappling them with more light than shade, but still, a welcome break from the unrelenting sun among the tiny peach trees.

Birdie, always kind, tried to make Grey feel at home. "Did you go to high school with Lee? I don't think I've ever seen you in town. I was homeschooled though. Ooh, look." Birdie swerved out of line to a bushy plant full of purple flowers. She plucked a few delightedly. "Lilacs." She thrust them toward Leeda's face, and Leeda smiled, sniffing. Birdie could make something exciting out of anything on the orchard. She knew all the flowers, the species of birds, how much rainfall they could expect, where moss was likely to grow, which mushrooms were edible, and how long many of the trees had been in the ground. To walk across the property with Birdie was never just to walk through unnoticed space. She offered the lilacs to Grey next, but he shook his head, and Birdie looked slightly rejected. Leeda frowned at the back of his neck.

Up ahead, Murphy came to an abrupt halt, bathed in the sun while the rest of them were still dotted by the shade. She threw her arms up in the air in an exaggerated stretch, her baggy jeans, rolled up above her knees, drooping so that the waist sagged below her hips. "Aah, lake."

She charged horselike down to the water while Leeda and the others just crested the clearing. Murphy was almost to where the lake lay like an inkblot. She teetered at the water's edge with one foot in the air like a stork, pulling off a black-and-white Puma, a sock, and then swiped at the water's surface with her toe, sending ripples emanating outward. Birdie smiled like lightning, blindingly bright, at both of them, and then she followed, kicking off her sandals and sinking down into the grass.

Grey stayed where he was, removed, holding tightly to the Chihuahua's leash as the dog tugged and strained to follow the girls. He kept throwing glances at Leeda and then looking away. Leeda decided it wasn't worth her time wondering why. She longed to follow her friends down to the water, which—this time of year—would still be cold despite the heat. But she hung back instead, not wanting to abandon a guest. She checked the ground carefully before sitting.

"Trying not to get dirty?" Grey asked.

"I'm looking for fire ants," she said evenly. She looked up at him and then pointed to her legs. All down the front of her shins were tiny white circular scars where she had been bitten one summer night.

Seeing that the area was safe, she knelt and began to unpack the picnic basket. The grass grew thin and fine and soft as fur here.

Grey stood awkwardly, his eyes still on the lake.

Leeda sighed, thinking any normal person would have made some effort to make conversation. She was at a loss as to how to talk to him.

"Would you like to sit down?" she asked.

He looked at her, then sat at the very edge of the blanket, like he couldn't be far enough away from her.

"It's great, isn't it?" she asked, thinking this was the most pleasant conversation topic she could come up with. "Birdie's farm?"

"I guess."

Leeda tightened her lips. "You could just say yes," she blurted out.

"Why?" Grey challenged her, finally looking interested and present.

"To be polite."

Grey squinted across the lawn. "What's so great about being polite? I'd rather be genuine."

Leeda got flustered for a moment. But then she laughed,

making sure he saw he wasn't upsetting her. "And being rude is genuine? Who raised you, wolves?"

Grey didn't reply.

Fuming, she started to unwrap the sandwiches. A few minutes later, after an agonizingly awkward silence, Birdie and Murphy came flopping up to them, half dry and half soaked, having done everything to get themselves wet except jump in the lake. Murphy lifted the bottom of her T-shirt to wipe her mud-splattered face. There wasn't a guy alive who hadn't checked Murphy out at some point or another, but Grey only stared down at the dog.

"So where are you from, Grey?" Murphy asked, too cavalier and restless to notice the tension between him and Leeda.

"Nowhere, really," he said, looking at the dog instead of Murphy. "I just got out of foster care when I turned eighteen." Leeda felt her throat tighten slightly. "I'm just moving around now."

Murphy cocked her head, intrigued and fascinated, while Leeda was just uncomfortable and unsure what to say. "Foster care, huh? What's that like?" Murphy pressed. Leeda shot her a look.

Grey shrugged coolly. "Depends on the family. I had three. They've been all right." It didn't seem like an emotionally deep topic for him. He seemed as bored by it as he did by everything else.

Leeda tried to picture moving into a family that had its own culture and personality completely separate from you. It sounded like being raised by wolves.

Grey bent forward and let the dog off its leash, then stood and started forward, taking off his shirt and dropping it on the grass. His back was pale. He walked down to the water's edge and waded in. The Chihuahua launched itself toward Majestic and the two dogs ran laps around the grass, like racecars sidling up to each other.

"He seems okay," Murphy said, her green eyes, always alert, on Grey. "Quiet, maybe. That's crazy he was a foster kid."

"Yeah," Birdie said. "He's not ugly either. You said he was ugly."

"I didn't say he was ugly," Leeda said. "Just mean."

"He doesn't look mean; he looks disappointed," Birdie said, scratching at her head. "He looks like a taller, very sad Jake Gyllenhaal."

"No way does he look like Jake Gyllenhaal," Murphy said. "Anyway, Bird, you think everyone who's mean is actually just sad."

"That's true," Birdie said, picking at some grass. Majestic and the Chihuahua zipped up to them, and Majestic barreled onto Birdie's lap. The Chihuahua settled nervously at Leeda's knee, staring up at her uncertainly, licking his lips, and then settling down onto his front paws.

Birdie had loaded a batch of June Princes into the basket, and Leeda cradled two to her chest, nibbling on a third. Eating a peach was a multilayered experience. It was soft and juicy, fuzzy, tough, and messy. It involved your fingers and cheeks getting slopped with juice.

"Why are you hoarding food?" Murphy said with her mouth full. Which was ironic, considering she had tackled the peaches greedily. She had a tiny bit of peach skin pasted to the side of her chin like a murder clue.

Birdie sank against Leeda's side, and Leeda combed the tangles out of her hair absently while Murphy watched Grey, who was doing strong, steady laps across the lake. Leeda felt contentment bubble up in her, suddenly intoxicating. It was a perfect day, and there was a light breeze, and she had the sweet feeling of being in the best place and the best moment she could possibly be in. She only felt these moments from time to time, and all of them that she could remember had happened at the orchard. She only wished Eric could be there too. She picked a twig from the ground and stuffed it into her pocket.

Leeda was studying a bee when a shadow suddenly fell upon her, and she looked up to where Grey was blocking the sun and pulling his shirt back on. He looked like he was thinking something over. Murphy and Birdie kept staring at him like he was some kind of TV show, waiting for what would happen next.

"Do you want something to eat?" Birdie asked.

"No thanks."

He looked at Leeda for a few seconds, long enough to make her uncomfortable. "I gotta go," he said.

He scooped up the leash and attached it to the Chihuahua, who was sitting on his hind legs now that Grey was back, waving at the air. But Grey only stood there awkwardly, his athletic body paused and still, as if he wanted to say something. Finally he spoke. "I'm sorry I was rude about your grandmom, Leeda."

And just like that, without a good-bye, Grey was on his way back into the peach rows.

They all watched him disappear into the space where the trees wove together.

"He's like Heathcliff from *Wuthering Heights*." Birdie sighed. "All moody."

"Well, he's definitely . . . special," Murphy said.

Leeda stared after him, bewildered. The last thing she saw was the Chihuahua, straining back toward her, before he too disappeared into the trees.

Thirteen

"Can you find me the tax stuff from last year?" Birdie's dad asked, leaning over his desk and fishing for a pen.

"Sure."

Birdie walked over to the shelves of her dad's office and expertly scanned the chaotic piles, zeroing in on a blue folder and sliding it out of the mess. Her dad had called her inside to help with paperwork. He sometimes did so when things outside were running smoothly, which, by mid-June, they often were. This was the first time she'd spent much time in the house since she'd moved into her tree house.

The office was a small square room, with dark walls and crooked shelves and the same warped, sunken floors that held up the rest of the house. There was an old TV in one corner that hadn't worked since the eighties. Knickknacks littered the shelves. They had no particular shelving system—they were the only two people who could find anything.

Birdie and her father had spent many days like this, working in tandem on orchard finances, poring over information about pesticides and fertilizer, calling Southern Counties Farm Supply to order anything they were low on. They had spent far more time together than most fathers and daughters, often holding the finances and the farm together by a thread. Birdie had always been eager to help, always excited to take over a job from her dad and take on more responsibility. By now, they were a well-oiled machine.

As she waited for her dad to hand her the next batch of work, she studied him. Birdie rarely looked at her dad—really looked at him. She looked at other people's dads, observed them objectively: the graying at their temples, whether they seemed strong or mellow or preoccupied. But she couldn't remember the last time she had looked at her dad with clear eyes. And now that she sat, gazing at him, he looked tired. Tired and stressed out. His hair had more white than other dads she knew. His hands were rougher from the farm work, and he had more wrinkles from spending so much time in the sun. Birdie's dad had given a lot to their farm, and the farm had taken things from him—his early mornings, his nights, all his time, really. It wasn't a place that allowed for days off. Nature kept moving whether you worked or not.

Birdie felt the same lost feeling opening at the pit of her stomach, so she stood and studied the messy shelves, looking for a distraction. There were huge tomes on trees and fruits, an old dictionary, cookbooks with their bindings coming apart, old photo albums, a couple of books on Bridgewater that included photos of the orchard and its "historic" house. "Historic" only because it was old.

She fished out one of the books and opened it to a well-worn page that featured the orchard. In this photo, black-and-white and grainy, a dark-haired woman stood in front of the house, smiling in a gray dress. The caption read, *Owner Mandie Rae Adlai, 1932.*

Mandie Rae's face was familiar to Birdie. It appeared in a couple of old photo albums that had come with the house itself and in a few histories of the town. Mandie Rae had abandoned the orchard, just up and left it one day. But Birdie had always felt a sympathetic connection to the pretty, petite woman in the photo. Like they were tied up by belonging to this place—like the orchard had been passed down like an heirloom between them. They were farm women, both of them. Mandie had given it up by choice, though. Birdie couldn't imagine doing the same.

"This is gonna take me a while," Walter said. "Why don't you go get yourself some lunch or something?"

Birdie nodded and padded into the hall, her socked feet sliding on the old, slippery wood floors.

Poopie was humming in the kitchen.

Birdie hovered in the archway. Ever since Enrico had failed to get off the bus, she had known she was going to have this conversation. And yet, she hadn't been able to start it. She had been torn, but she'd also felt it was inevitable. And thinking about it was the only thing that had soothed her.

"Um, Poopie, can I talk to you?"

Poopie gave her a look, and then closed her book on her lap.

"Enrico and I . . . we aren't getting married."

Poopie nodded slowly. "I know. Of course, Avelita." She smiled gently and turned, pressing her back against the counter. She had flour on her hands, and she looked tired too. She waited for Birdie to say more.

"I don't have this . . . other life. I never really did." Birdie cleared her throat.

Poopie nodded. Birdie's heart fluttered. She hesitated, and then forced herself to spit it out.

"I don't want you to sell the orchard."

Poopie nodded again at the floor, unsurprised.

A lot of things moved around inside Birdie now that the words were out. Relief. Guilt. Giddy hope. "I know you have all these plans. And it'll be a lot of work for you. But I need you to wait until I'm done with school. Then . . ." Birdie swallowed. "Then you can go wherever you want. I'll be ready to move home and take over."

Poopie only watched her and listened.

"There's this thing I feel inside when I think about not having this place," Birdie said, and a lump got stuck in her throat. "It feels terrible."

She was going to say more, but she realized there wasn't anything more to it. Poopie was silent. She looked at her hands. Then finally she came across the room, took Birdie's hand, and stared into her eyes.

"Look." She thrust a finger toward the sagging line of the doors, the slanted floor. "A hundred years of sinking right into the ground."

Birdie studied the door frames. Most of the doors in the house hadn't been properly closable in years. Birdie could roll marbles down the floor. The furnace often broke in the winter. The windows were drafty.

"I know," Birdie said. "I know it's decrepit. But I'd be lost without this place."

Poopie studied her hard. Her face scrunched into little, thoughtful lines. "I don't know how, but I'll talk to your father about what we might be able to do," she finally said.

Birdie felt relief flood through her. Poopie reached her arms around her and squeezed tightly, and Birdie sank into the hug.

A few minutes later, Birdie stepped outside and back into the gray, overcast day. The workers had deserted the fields for lunch, and she could hear their familiar sounds through the trees. She walked down to the lake and, even though it was a little too chilly, stripped down to her skivvies and waded into the water. It had a gloomy coolness to it, but she liked it. It shocked her skin and cleared her head.

Birdie had tons of little rituals like this, all through the orchard, that she could turn to when her soul was sore or weary: a hollow oak tree into which she could crawl and count the termites, a tiny rise on the northwestern perimeter where she could sit and be completely alone with a bit of a view of the trees.

She lay back in the water and floated. She didn't separate from her surroundings in any way. They were like part of her own body. She couldn't leave the orchard, and it couldn't leave her.

She heard a muffled voice and drew herself back up out of the water, her toes making contact with the mud underneath her feet. Her hair dripped down her back.

Poopie stood on the shore.

"Your father says it's up to you," she said. "He said we won't take the house down if you don't say it's okay."

Birdie felt her heart soar, and she beamed.

"But Birdie, we think that when you have thought on everything, you will see that it is the only thing to do. And so we aren't going to say anything to the workers yet. They will still think it's the last summer. If, in the end, it changes"—Poopie shrugged—"we will invite them back and hope for the best."

Birdie's spirits sank a little, but as Poopie turned and walked back up toward the trees, heading for the house, mostly Birdie felt relief.

I can fix this. I can fix my house, she thought. She ducked back under the water to sweep her hair out of her face and came up again, refreshed. It was like she was being baptized.

Fourteen

The Dooly County Fair was in the town of Nomini Creek, sixty miles from Bridgewater down a winding back road. Leeda sat in silence in the passenger seat of Grey's truck, sipping a cup of coffee from the Circle K and watching the scenery go by—the scraggly trees surrounding downtown Bridgewater transitioning into thick, deep woods on both sides of the road. Compared to northern woods, which Leeda had seen on a trip up the Hudson River Valley, the Georgia forest felt primeval. Northern trees seemed picturesque and petite to Leeda, their leaves small in soft, bright greens. Georgia forests were loaded with tall, drooping trees covered in kudzu and smothered in deep greens that seemed like they could swallow someone up. Leeda had never noticed it before.

She and Grey had barely exchanged more than hellos when she'd arrived at the cottage just after dawn that morning. Now, staring out the window, she was trying to wake up, occasionally looking back at the long silver trailer hooked to the back of the truck to make sure that it—and The Baron and Sneezy inside it—hadn't disappeared. A few wrinkled books littered the backseat. Something by someone named Immanuel Kant. A book called

The Fabric of the Cosmos. A Tom Clancy novel, the cover curled back like a ribbon.

"So you took the dog back?" she finally asked, ending the silence.

"Yeah." Grey nodded. Leeda felt a pang, but she quickly rationalized that it had been out of her hands. There had been nothing else she could do.

Grey was a good driver—focused, with quick reflexes. He swerved slowly to miss a snake slithering across the road, spotting it from several yards away.

"So you didn't go to college or anything?" Leeda asked haltingly, glancing again at the books in the backseat. She'd been dying to ask since the day at the lake.

"No." He shook his head. "I could have gotten loans. But I'm just not very interested."

"And you just . . . drift around?"

Grey nodded. It sounded kind of pointless to Leeda, but she didn't say so. "That must be very nice," she said instead. But Grey seemed to sense the insincerity, and he frowned.

"Why do you want to do marketing?" he asked after a minute.

"Because . . ." Leeda thought about saying what she usually said to her relatives. Something about room to grow. Something with the word *dynamic* in it. "I guess because I can move on to an MA in business afterward. That's what my parents want," she admitted, smiling sheepishly. "But I don't want to just give in completely."

"You're planning your life around what your parents want? Don't you think that's kind of vapid?" he asked, sounding a little disgusted.

Leeda was taken off guard. "It's practical," she said defensively.

"Is doing something soulless being practical?"

"It's not soulless . . ." she argued, feeling her face flush. "It's—"

"Being a cog in a wheel isn't soulless?" Grey asked, not letting her finish.

Leeda's fingers tightened into fists on her lap. "Could you be any more cliché?" she asked. He didn't answer. She let out an annoyed sigh and turned as tightly as she could toward the window. "I'll take your thoughts into account while I'm planning my life, Karl Marx."

Grey just drove on calmly, and his continued silence infuriated her further. Like he'd provoked her emotions, and then removed himself by a thousand mental miles.

"Anyway, I don't see how you're doing anything so great by being a pony guy and . . . whatever else. It's so easy to say what I should or shouldn't do with my time when you're not really doing anything with yours."

Grey rolled down the window and hung his arm out, completely ignoring her. Leeda wanted to reach across the seat and push him out the door. Instead she raised her chin and glared at the forest.

When they pulled into the parking lot of the fair, she poured herself out of the truck fast as a waterfall and went back to check on the ponies. Sneezy and The Baron both stared at her. The Baron let out a huffy, nasally sound.

She reached out to pat his muzzle, but he jerked away irritably, as if he sensed Leeda's bad mood. That's what she'd always thought about animals. That they knew your soul. And something about Leeda's turned them off.

The fair sprawled out across a hundred acres of booths, dusty lots, and grassy fields, the Ferris wheel and the Salt and Pepper Shaker hanging above it all, the smell of hay and funnel cakes woven through the air. Grey led both ponies expertly off the trailer, and they each took ahold of one by the halter. Leeda pulled The Baron along awkwardly with Grey and Sneezy leading the way. She just hoped the pony didn't bite her.

By the time they crossed the lot to their booth—in a huge maze of booths where all the livestock was gathered—Leeda was sweaty, covered in a thin layer of dust, and irritable.

They set up the ponies with water and alfalfa, Leeda taking cues from Grey. Finally they were situated and stood with their hands on their hips, surveying the bustling crowds around them.

For the next hour or so, they casually ignored each other, leaning on the wall of the pony pen, staring out at the people who drifted by.

"You mind if I wander off and explore for a while?" Grey finally asked.

Leeda was relieved. "No. Go ahead."

After he was gone, Leeda turned and looked at the ponies, who stared at her accusingly. She leaned her chin on her hands and watched the action go by—farmers with their kids, a lot of overweight people eating giant portions of greasy food, people in all the same kinds of outfits—jeans from the Gap, American Eagle T-shirts, and the like—anything easily found at the local mall.

She thought about Grey. What he'd said in the car rankled her, making her stomach ache. She kept finding herself holding her breath.

She didn't feel vapid, she argued in her head. Vapid seemed empty, and Leeda swirled inside much of the time. And she felt full of love and appreciation for things. She felt worry, too. But still, it felt like he'd peeled back a piece of her, hitting on something that sometimes scared her.

When she was little, her dad had read her *Pinocchio* many times before bed. Leeda still thought about the story a lot, in moments when she was sad or lying in bed, her defenses down before falling asleep. What worried her, sometimes, was that she had never been able to capture the feeling of being completely real. Even in New York, she hadn't quite been able to catch the elusive feeling she thought she should have of being complete.

Remembering New York made her realize she'd momentarily forgotten it. Leeda dug into her pocket, pulled out her cell phone, and hit two on the speed dial. Eric answered on the first ring.

"Hey stranger."

"Hey." Leeda picked at the fence of the pen. "I'm sorry I haven't called. It's crazy busy here."

"I figured."

They were quiet for a second, missing each other. Leeda could hear street noise in the background on Eric's end, and she longed for the dreamlike excitement of the city. "Hey, can I ask you something?" Leeda said.

"Sure."

"Do you think I'm vapid?"

"What?"

"I don't know. I just . . . Do you ever feel like you don't know who you are?"

"Leeda, I know who you are. You are not vapid. You're wonderful. You're smart. You're beautiful. You've got so much going for you; trust me."

Leeda took it in, just listening in silence. It wasn't quite what she needed to know. But she didn't know how to ask for what she did.

They talked about the last couple of days, and about plans, and about Leeda's estimated date for her return to New York, which was getting fuzzier and fuzzier all the time. "I don't know, maybe the first week in July," she said. She couldn't believe they were already even talking about July.

Eric was disappointed but supportive. "Hey, I love you, Lee," he said when she'd been quiet for a few moments.

"I love you too," she said into the phone. She met Sneezy's eyes as they said their good-byes, and she hung up.

She smiled at the pony, like a peace offering, as if the animal could understand smiling. The pony just stared at her and, embarrassed, Leeda glanced away. Looking into the booth next to her, she noticed a display of baby chicks hatching in a big, clear plastic incubator. It was an agonizingly slow process—tiny little pecks, the occasional hairline crack, the eventual collapsing of a small piece of shell. And some of the chicks didn't make it. A few of them died right there, before they made it all the way out. But the ones that did were fuzzy and cute, stumbling about, snuggling together.

When she turned back, Sneezy was still staring at her expectantly with her big brown eyes. Leeda reached out and gently touched Sneezy on the tip of the nose. The pony let out a warm breath that tickled her hand. Leeda let her hand fall and turned to watch the crowds again.

A couple of people took the business cards she'd had printed up at Kinko's. But no one seemed seriously excited about Sneezy or The Baron.

Eventually Grey reappeared. They silently watched the dusk descend and the lights of the rides and the vendors go on in bright whites and pinks. From somewhere across the grounds, the night's entertainment boomed in faraway notes and indecipherable words, reverberating through the dusty field. At around 8 p.m., when no one had stopped by the booth for an hour, they started to pack up.

It was late when Leeda and Grey pulled into the driveway of Primrose Cottage, the sound of the tires on the white paving stones interrupting the sound of the crickets. It had been a long, quiet ride, and Leeda was sleepy as she slid out of the truck and climbed the porch stairs into the house, leaving Grey to unload the ponies and bring them to the barn. She didn't feel like getting back in her car and driving to the orchard.

To the left of the parlor, a door opened into one of the spare bedrooms where Grey had been sleeping. Leeda walked to the doorway and peered in. Grey's belongings were few: a big duffel bag with a pile of dirty clothes inside, a canvas painting of bicyclists racing, a tiny bag with his toothbrush and razor. It smelled like boy's deodorant, sweet and masculine. Leeda turned back to the parlor and listened to the clock tick. She imagined that, on many nights, Grandmom Eugenie must have had only this sound to listen to.

Leeda walked upstairs to the bedroom and changed into one of her grandmom's old nightgowns, which felt a little spooky. She sat on the bed dangling her feet, feeling sleepy and restless simultaneously.

She stared at her grandmother's bureau. She thought about the letter she'd found. And then she popped up from the bed and walked across the carpet. Slowly, she pulled the first drawer open. But when that turned up empty of anything but old control-top panty hose and underwear, she got bolder, opening drawer after drawer, losing her compunction. Next she turned to the closet, searching the shoe boxes on the shelf at the top, and then turning to the boxes down below. On the third box, she hit it. She slid the box out of the closet and put it on the bed, opening it up. There had to be forty letters, tied together with a white ribbon and all addressed to Eugenie in the same hand with no return address. Leeda opened the first few—some were simply letters that planned out meeting times. *Oak tree, 7 p.m. Swimming tonight.* Others were longer, telling small stories about things that had happened in the course of a few days, and some were just full of sweetness, teasing Eugenie for her quirky, eccentric little ways or expressing longing and tenderness.

One, Leeda kept coming back to. It wasn't dated. But it was toward the end of the pile, and the things it said seemed to be a culmination of all the things before.

Genie,

I'm sorry for the other night. I know by now that trying to push you into anything makes you get farther away from it. I don't know why I think trying to reason with you will work. Sometimes I just hope you'll be open, and human, and hear me, just because it's important to me and for no other reason.

I know there's too much in the way between you and me. But I also know that when I'm with you, it's like something more than being in my body. It's like a piece of my soul isn't inside me anymore, but it's all wrapped up wherever you are. It's one of the things in this world that makes me believe people are more than just skin and bones. That when I'm with you, I feel like someone and something bigger than what I thought.

Genie, I'm gonna ask you one more time. Please don't do what you're planning to do. Do the impossible thing instead. Be with me. Be brave and be with me.

Your M.

Leeda lingered over the words, touching them with her fingers, and then dug at the bottom of the box for anything left over. It was as if she didn't know how the whole thing had ended. It was like she hoped it would end differently. There was one final note, the folds worn, as if it had been opened and folded many times. It was brief.

Genie,

I'll wait for you tonight, you know where. And I know it's spoiling the surprise, but I bought you a ring. Isn't that the silliest thing? It cost me every last drop of my savings. And I know

you would never wear it. And nobody would ever understand it.
But the thing is, I have a life ahead of me that doesn't involve
watching you marry somebody else. So I'm going to leave tomor-
row, either way. Tonight you need to decide. Are you coming?

♥ *M.*

Leeda folded up the letter like it had been and carefully
replaced all of them in their box. She felt heavy and exhausted.
She hadn't read one word written by her grandmother, but the
weight of her suffering had come through on every page. Leeda
felt, most of all, her grandmom's fear in the face of her lover's
courage. He had been begging her to do the brave thing. And
apparently, marrying Leeda's grandfather had been the easier
choice, though Leeda didn't know why.

Leeda wondered whether her grandmom had thought about
someone finding her letters in the closet after she died. Surely
she knew that if she kept them, they would be found eventually.
It wasn't like she had died a spring chicken.

But she had left the house to Leeda for as long as she had the
ponies. Had she thought Leeda would find them? Did she want
her to? And did she want Lucretia to know? Did she want everyone to know? Did she care?

It seemed that, after years of keeping secrets, Eugenie would
have had some plan for the evidence she had left behind. But
Leeda had never known her well enough to guess what her inten-
tions could have been.

She stood and slid the box back into the closet. Then she
shuffled into the bathroom to brush her teeth. Back in the bed-

room, she pulled back the covers and crawled underneath, turning off the lamp beside the bed. The light coming through the window illuminated the room, reminding her there was a full moon.

Leeda laid her head back on the pillow, and her mind drifted rapidly but aimlessly to the baby chicks that never got a chance, and to Grey being alone once he turned eighteen, and to the poor doomed love of her grandmother. It was a long time before she came back to herself and remembered that no one but her was in the room, and much of what she was thinking of was now in the past. She was only a girl lying in a quiet house with the moonlight on her bed.

Fifteen

The Bridgewater Courthouse was lit up in the summer sun; the reflection off it was so bright that Murphy shielded her eyes as she climbed out of the truck she'd borrowed from the Darlingtons. The air smelled like hot tar and melted grape Blow Pop. Murphy squinted at the large wooden front doors, and then at the clock hanging above them. Quarter to three.

Murphy had no romantic notions about finding her father. She wasn't looking for a hug, or any *Oprah*-type crying, or hours spent reconnecting. She didn't want him in her life, and she respected that he had chosen freedom over her. Most girls would have been angry or angst-ridden that their dads had skipped out when they were babies. But when Murphy had thought of her dad at all, she had always hoped he was off somewhere living exactly the life he wanted. She understood his desire to be unfettered. She had been sure that, if nothing else, that was something she had inherited from him.

The discovery that he existed in some real, connected way had just made her want to see him; that was all. She knew Jodee was meeting him here. She just wanted to lay eyes on him.

She had gone with Birdie to her mom's for lunch and had left Birdie there. Now Murphy sat at a spindly picnic table on the grass at the side of the lot, playing nickel basketball with herself in the sun. It was no easy task, and between failed shots she glanced up at the courthouse. She was out of the way enough to be unseen, but close enough to see everyone coming and going.

One of her friends in New York worked at a Starbucks. He'd said that during training, they were told to try to make Starbucks a customer's "third place." Home. Work. Starbucks. In response, Murphy had turned her fingers into devil horns and told the guy that Starbucks was the devil. But if Murphy had a "third place," it was here at the courthouse. She knew the schedules of the two receptionists who worked there. She could have written the biography of Judge Abbott—how, though he was probably only her mom's age, he was graying at the temples, jowly, and serious-faced. How he wore shiny Payless loafers, was an upstanding citizen, and liked to tap his feet to the beat of "Row, Row, Row Your Boat" when he was listening to testimony from Murphy's various accusers—Bob's Big Boy for stealing their mascot, Kmart for stealing underwear, the town council for replacing all the framed pictures of the legislators in their hallway with pictures of players from the Orlando Magic.

Now a rumble drew her eyes to the road, where her mom's Pontiac was just pulling into the parking lot. Murphy slunk closer to the picnic table even though she didn't need to. As Jodee got out of her car, she barely looked where she was walking as she made her way into the courthouse.

A few moments later, another car followed—a green Chrysler LeBaron. Murphy leaned forward. A moment ago she had been perfectly relaxed, still not quite believing this would actually happen. Now her heart fluttered in her chest. She leaned rigidly into the picnic table.

A man got out of the car. He was wearing jeans and a burgundy-colored T-shirt. He was tall, with dark brown hair and green eyes. Murphy took in everything about him—his skin, his shoes, whether or not there were bumper stickers on his car. (There was one. It said, nonsensically, MY OTHER CAR IS A BROOM.) She sent up a silent prayer that he wouldn't have one of those "peeing Calvins" of Calvin and Hobbes stickers on his back windshield. Thankfully, she didn't see one.

Murphy knew she should feel emotional, but she didn't. She didn't feel connected to the man crossing the lot. She just felt eager to know. And eager to keep a safe distance.

He walked casually, as if he didn't have a care in the world, as if he wasn't on the way to a paternity hearing. In another moment, he was gone, disappearing through the double doors.

Murphy pulled away from the table and walked over to her truck. She got in and waited, sinking low in the seat but keeping her eyes on the door.

Half an hour later, the man reemerged with Judge Abbott and Murphy's mom. They all separated, Judge Abbott walking in the direction of town and Jodee and Murphy's dad heading to their respective cars.

He walked to his car and got in, pulling out of his parking spot and pausing at the exit. Murphy started the engine.

She hadn't planned on doing it. But when the LeBaron pulled onto Main Street, Murphy pulled out behind him.

They had been on I-95 North for about twenty miles when he finally pulled off at a familiar exit. But instead of heading into the residential area of the town, he turned left, finally parking at a bar called Buckets.

Murphy looked at the clock. Four-thirty p.m. *That's my dad, all right*, she thought.

She watched him walk inside.

Now was her chance. She could follow him in. Say hi. Introduce herself. Ask him a thing or two. What was his favorite drink? Was he as free as he wanted to be? What places had he been to? What did she have that came from him? Or she could drive away. Put it behind her. Possibly never see him again.

Murphy wasn't ready to talk to him. But she wasn't ready to give him up forever either. She idled for several minutes, debating with herself. And then she turned the truck around toward Bridgewater.

On the way back, the whole event got bigger in her mind. She regretted not going in. She worried he was gone for good. And she needed to know. She needed to know if being unfettered had been worth it for him.

Bridgewater looked small as Murphy turned off the exit ramp. She felt no attachment to the town itself. But it did look pretty while driving in—beyond the fast-food joints that greeted her at first, downtown was small and quaint.

Instead of heading toward the orchard, she turned toward home. She would confront her mom with what she'd seen. Murphy wouldn't let her deny it.

Her headlights, as she turned in, swept the lot of Anthill Acres Trailer Park and her own front stairs. Two figures were standing outside her mother's trailer, talking. Murphy stopped the car, frozen in place.

The man reached out for Jodee, and Jodee gave him a tight hug and thanked him loudly. They said good-bye, and Jodee disappeared into the house. The man continued down the stairs toward his truck, got in, and started the engine.

Murphy only could gape at him as he pulled out onto the street. Not before he looked both ways, of course.

Rex always was a careful driver.

Sixteen

"*H*e's staying at the Homewood Suites," Murphy said. She was standing in the doorway of the cider shed, looking incredulous, her arms hanging at her sides. Birdie, a crate of peaches midair and ready to pour into the press, squinted at her.

"Rex?"

"Yep." Murphy nodded. "The guy at Circle K told me."

It was a misty, cool day, and even though it was noon, it was still dim and felt early. The mist had infiltrated Murphy's hair and had made it twice as puffy as usual. It felt like they were somewhere remote and alone.

Overcast days were always blessings at the orchard. As long as the picking wasn't interrupted, they were a pleasant escape from the relentless sun and heat. And if rain began, picking ended for the day, and the workers retreated to the dorms to relax, play cards, talk, watch TV, and hang out. Everything slowed down.

"That's crazy. Why hasn't he come to see you?" Murphy had told Birdie what she'd seen the other night and that she'd planned to sleuth it all out. Murphy had taken on an air of cool determination that, Birdie knew, never boded well.

"Why's he going to see my mom?" Murphy asked.

A weird, awkward thought hung between both of them. Jodee McGowen had always been crazy about Rex. And she was single. And she had dated younger guys before. But Birdie quickly dismissed the thought as ludicrous and hoped that Murphy had done the same.

The sound of damp footsteps and voices announced someone approaching, and Murphy turned as Emma and Raeka appeared beside her in the doorway with crates of peaches.

"I'm gonna go up to the tree house," Murphy said to Birdie. "I'll see you up there in a bit." She waved to the two women and left.

Emma and Raeka sidled up beside Birdie and began dumping their peaches into the press. Birdie watched Raeka's strong hands.

"Hey, I wanted to ask you guys something," Birdie said in English. Some things were too important to her to communicate in a foreign language. And now that she had them alone, she felt it was a rare opportunity. Her gut throbbed a little. "How was Enrico when you left?"

Emma and Raeka came from Enrico's town in Mexico. They knew him well.

Raeka ran a wrist across her forehead to wipe back her damp hair and smiled at Birdie knowingly and sympathetically.

"He was okay."

"Do you hear anything about him?" Birdie swallowed. "Does he have a new girlfriend or anything?"

Emma grinned sadly. "You don't want him to move on, Birdie?"

But Raeka was shaking her head. "It's not that easy, Birdie. Nobody is allowed to talk about you," Raeka said. "He just locks himself up with his chicken and listens to music, and he doesn't want to hear your name." Emma nodded along, her eyes wide for emphasis.

Birdie flicked her thumbnails against each other, staring at them dismally.

"Oh, Birdie." Raeka reached her hand to Birdie's face and squeezed her chin. "You are young. You will be in love again, maybe many times. It's okay to let it go."

Birdie found the thought nauseating. "I don't want many more loves."

Raeka nodded. Birdie knew she had divorced two years ago. She felt like a broken engagement was a small loss compared to that. But they were both pampering her, as always.

Emma squeezed Birdie's shoulder before she and Raeka turned and headed outside again.

Birdie wasn't far behind them. Once she was done with the day's cider, pressing it and pouring the juice into jugs assembly-line style, she stored the jugs in a corner of the shed and walked outside, trudging toward her tree house. The damp grass wet Birdie's feet as she walked, and the sound of tiny raindrops on thousands of leaves sounded like static. When she was almost there she noticed a figure coming toward her across the soggy grass. Birdie was only a couple of feet away before she realized it was Horatio Balmeade.

"Hey, Birdie." He stopped, grinning with his white, white teeth. "How are you? I hear you've been on all sorts of adventures."

"Yeah." She shuffled her feet a couple of times. "Are you looking for my dad?"

"We're meeting about an offer I'm making on the place. Looks promising."

Birdie hardened into stone. Mr. Balmeade waited for her to say something, and when she didn't, he adjusted his straw fedora. "Well, I think we'll all be pretty happy." He raised a hand in the air. "I'll see you." With the same manufactured smile, he walked on past her up toward the house.

Birdie's mind reeled. She felt a rug had just been pulled out from under her. But instead of heading up to the house, she practically ran the rest of the way to her tree, climbing the ladder two rungs at a time. The edges of the platform were wet with rain where there was no overhang. Murphy and Leeda had brought over snacks. Leeda sat with her pen poised over paper, drafting letters to prospective pony adopters.

"We brought you some peach cookies—" Murphy said, but her mouth froze in a questioning O when she saw Birdie's face.

Birdie held her breath for a moment. And then she let out a long string of obscenities, enraged half sentences, names, and words disembodied from any kind of context.

She paced from one end of the platform to the other, as if her words made it impossible for her not to move, not to wave her arms to her ranting, in time. The looks of utter shock on Leeda's and Murphy's faces only fueled the fire.

As she went on, something drew the girls' attention away from her, but Birdie didn't care—she only got louder.

"What's he doing here?" Leeda murmured, looking down.

Birdie whipped around to look too, but at the same moment she lost her balance, teetering on the edge of the platform. She waved her arms frantically.

The last thing she saw was Grey running toward the base of the tree, reaching out as if he might catch her.

Seventeen

"You sure you're gonna be okay, Bird?" Leeda asked.

Birdie nodded, wincing and holding her calf. Poopie and Walter were sitting beside her, Uncle Walter looking at his daughter with worry. Birdie's mom was on her way, and Murphy was finding a vending machine. Grey, miraculously unscathed, stood behind Leeda.

Birdie looked embarrassed. Poopie had explained exasperatedly, on the way over, that Walter wasn't selling to Horatio Balmeade, and that he had intended to turn him down in the meeting. Now, huddled on the hard emergency-room chair, Birdie looked apologetic and pained at the same time. Leeda felt for her.

"You go on, Leeda," Uncle Walter said. "We'll take good care of her. It's probably just a sprain." He reached out his hand to shake Grey's. "It was nice to meet you."

"You too."

Leeda and Grey walked out into the hallway and down to the parking lot where Grey's truck was waiting.

He had explained to her on the way to the hospital that

Sneezy had colic, and he needed her help. He'd tried her on her BlackBerry, but when Leeda had seen it was Grey calling, she'd ignored it. That's why he'd come to the orchard.

"So I don't understand," Leeda said. "What's colic? And why can't we have a vet out?"

"It's a big deal for horses. It's basically constipation, but the thing is that to try to soothe the pain, they sometimes roll. And rolling, when they're all blocked up like that, can burst their intestines."

Leeda winced. In her head, she cursed her grandmother for leaving her the ponies. She didn't want to deal with a pony that might die. Grey drove fast, and it worried her all the more.

When they arrived at the corral, several of the ponies were up at the fence looking jittery, their ears pointed forward and their fur spiky. Leeda's eyes swept the field as she crossed the lawn behind Grey. She gasped when she saw a lump over toward the trees. Grey was already hauling himself over the fence. She followed, her shirt snagging on one of the nails as she tried ineptly to climb over.

Sneezy was on her left side. Leeda breathed a sigh of relief to see her eyes open and her chest moving, although her breath was extremely labored. She yanked her shirt off the nail and crossed the lot, standing beside the pony, helpless.

"We gotta get her up. We can't let her roll."

Leeda pictured intestines bursting and started to feel a little light-headed.

"Leeda, come on." Grey was gesturing to the pony's back. "I'll pull the head; you push her off her side toward her feet."

Leeda nodded, kneeling on the ground, feeling all thumbs

and totally graceless. When Grey gave the signal, she heaved. For something miniature, Sneezy was incredibly heavy, and she merely sank back against Leeda's hands.

"Again—one, two, three."

He pulled and Leeda pushed, and this time Sneezy seemed to become suddenly alert. She tottered up, first onto her hind legs, then straightening her front legs out underneath herself.

Leeda shot a bright, relieved smile at Grey, but he looked only slightly mollified.

"Okay, we need to walk her until she goes."

"Goes?"

Grey looked at her like she had to be kidding, and she suddenly caught his drift. "We should take turns," he said.

He grabbed Sneezy's halter and started walking her rapidly in a big circle, passing Leeda again and then continuing, pulling Sneezy along at a clipped pace. Suddenly the pony's back legs began to buckle, and he yanked on her bridle hard, smacking her on the shoulders.

"Why are you hitting her?"

"We've just got to keep her up."

He pulled the pony along again. "When I pass the rope off to you, you need to keep her moving. If you start going slowly, she'll try to lie down on you."

"Okay." Leeda nodded.

"Okay, next go-around I'll hand you the rope. You ready?"

"Yeah." Leeda swallowed. She knew she was the worst person possible for the job. But there was nobody else.

Grey handed her the rope, and she launched into a fast walk, like she was taking a torch in a relay. It hadn't been obvious when she was watching, but there was a fair amount of resistance, and within one circle Leeda was already getting tired.

"You've got to pull hard," Grey said.

"I'm pulling hard," she replied, but she felt ungainly and awkward and like she was going too slowly.

The pony began to resist harder, but Leeda barely noticed until she was suddenly pulled backward a step, and she turned to see that Sneezy's back legs had tucked underneath her and her rear was almost on the ground. Leeda tried to pull, but it was too late and her arms were too weak. Sneezy went all the way down, hitting the ground with a thud and beginning to roll back onto her side.

Grey was there that second, hitting the ground behind her and pushing against her back. Leeda let herself be pulled down with the halter.

"Pull her up by the chin," he grunted, and Leeda tucked her hands under the pony's chin, reaching for the bottom strap of her halter and feeling the soft sweaty fur of her throat, the veins straining as she panted. Sneezy's chest was moving up and down in short little bursts, like someone hyperventilating, her warm breath on Leeda's arms. Her eyes were unfocused.

Leeda began to pull, but though Sneezy's chin came up, everything from her shoulders down stayed put. Grey had turned and was pushing his back against her, digging his heels into the dirt.

"I don't know if you have enough arm strength. We should switch," Grey said. He nodded for Leeda to come to where he was, and she tripped over beside him. He put his hands on both her shoulders for expediency, shifting her so that her hands were on Sneezy's back, and then he moved in a flash to where Leeda had been and grabbed the halter.

Leeda could feel sweat as the muscles of the pony's back moved under her hands. Grey looked at her. "Ready? Push!"

Digging her knees into the dirt, she pushed with all her strength. They both did, and nothing happened. Leeda looked at Grey. He looked panicked. They tried twice more.

Finally, exhausted, Leeda let out a breath and collapsed gently against Sneezy's back. When she looked up, Grey was rubbing the pony's ears. His face was open, upset.

They rested for a couple of minutes, and then Grey nodded to her and they positioned themselves and heaved again. Nothing. Only Sneezy's breath sounded slower and more relaxed. Her eyes began to flutter. She got still.

"No," Grey said. Leeda moved her arm across the soft fur, resting her hand where she could feel Sneezy's heartbeat, in awe. Was she dying? Was Leeda holding something that was about to die?

She felt both awed and panicked. Her mind raced. She had read in books, as a kid, about horses and girls having deep connections, like they could almost read each other's minds. What would ponies want to live for? Starry nights. Hay. Breezes. She tried to think those things for Sneezy.

Grey wrapped his hands around the halter again and began to pull. "C'mon, Sneezy. C'mon, girl." Leeda began to push too, but hopelessly.

And then, a shuddering movement ran through the pony. The way she moved was unlike any other four-legged creature—her legs unfolded like spider legs, and she shifted backward and forward until suddenly, she was standing.

Leeda jumped back. Grey wasted no time. He yanked the pony forward into a walk and looked at Leeda like they'd just dodged a bullet.

They took turns again, walking her around the corral in circle after circle. Grey stayed with Leeda when she was pulling the halter, hovering close to Sneezy's rear in case she tried to go down again. But a few moments later Leeda heard a few soft thuds and turned to see a big pile of manure.

Grey put a hand to his face and let out a breath. "Thank God."

Leeda laughed under her breath, her shoulders relaxing, her whole body going soft and warm and a giddiness moving up her throat. "I never thought I'd be so happy to see a pile of poo," she said.

"Ha."

They walked her for another ten minutes. Finally Grey slowed Sneezy down, rubbing his hands along her muzzle, and looked at Leeda. "She's most likely out of danger now. We can get her in the stable and keep an eye on her there."

Leeda trailed behind him and the pony, stepping on manure but only vaguely noticing, she was so happy and exhausted. Once Grey had led Sneezy into her stall, he showed Leeda how to fill up her water bucket, and he spread some fresh straw on the ground. Then he leaned against the thin wooden wall opposite the stall and sank down, rubbing at his face to wake himself up, smearing more dirt across his cheeks than was already there.

"Somebody should probably stay with her awhile," he said. "You can go inside and go to sleep if you want."

"No, I'll hang out a bit," she said. She leaned against the wall too and melted down like taffy.

They were quiet, comfortably. Leeda was so exhausted it felt heavenly to just breathe.

After sitting for a while, Grey looked at her sideways, rubbed his whiskers with his fingers, and smirked, but in a harmless, companionable way.

"So why'd your grandmom leave you ponies?"

Leeda considered the question. "No idea."

"Because you said you weren't into animals."

Leeda smiled slightly. "I know."

He thought. "I can't figure it out. What *are* you into?"

Leeda looked at her knees, ran her palms over them. "I don't know," she said. After a few moments of silence, she went on, too tired and at the same time too full of life to be reserved. "I don't know what music I like. I just buy whatever clothes the magazines tell me to. I don't know what I want to be." She smiled sadly. "I don't know if I like muffins or cupcakes better."

Grey didn't answer. He just gazed at her thoughtfully. Leeda felt like she'd said something extremely revealing, even though she hadn't said much at all. She moved her thumbs back and forth against each other self-consciously.

Sneezy snorted. Grey looked at Leeda reluctantly, and then got up to stand beside her. Leeda followed. He ran his hands over the pony's ears. "She's still stressed," he said, his dark brows furrowing above his eyes.

Now that they weren't in a life-or-death situation, Leeda wanted to touch the pony but didn't quite know how. She wondered if

Sneezy had read any of her thoughts. Maybe she'd sensed that Leeda wasn't all bad.

Grey studied her for a moment. "Why don't you pet her? She likes to be petted here." Leeda placed her hands, where he indicated, on Sneezy's forehead. "You can feel where she likes you to touch her and where she doesn't. She'll let you know."

Leeda ran her fingers along the ridges, feeling where the pony's skull changed under her fur, feeling the sweat and the grains of dust stuck to her coat, the muscles of her shoulder blades, the strength of her neck. Sneezy swiveled her ears back and forth like satellites, listening to Leeda, to Grey, to Leeda, to Grey.

"I ran over Birdie's dog," Leeda blurted out. "Last year. I killed her."

Grey, surprisingly, smiled at her. It was the first time he had ever smiled at her. It was a kind, open smile.

Leeda ran her hands around the side of Sneezy's neck, down to her chest. Sneezy raised her nose to Leeda's cheek and breathed onto it gently. Leeda leaned forward and touched her cheek against the pony's snout.

"See, you're friends now," Grey said. Leeda smiled. It felt good. Warm and a little scary and good.

They were quiet for a while, until finally Leeda turned her face to him. "Where are you going in August?" she asked suddenly.

"Alaska. I'm gonna work on a fishing boat."

"That sounds hard."

He shrugged. "It's something new. I think odd jobs are my niche. I don't do all that well staying in one place." He smiled a little sheepishly. "I always think there's a place that's going to feel right. Like, maybe the next place. Like, home sweet home or something, and everyone's going to be perfect and good and not out for each other and petty and all that."

Leeda picked up her hands and dusted them off.

"I guess if you're really wise, though, you can make the kind of life you want wherever you are." He was quiet, and then seemed to shake it off. "So maybe being permanently dissatisfied is my niche. Which, now that we're on the subject, I'm really sorry about. I mean, I'm sorry for giving you such a hard time before. I do that, and it's like I can't stop myself." He lifted a foot and pressed it against the opposite wall. "I underestimate people's souls sometimes. I think you're right. It's easy to judge. But I don't know. I'm much better when you get to know me. I mean, I have friends and everything, scattered around." He smirked. "I'm not a total tosser."

Leeda nodded to let him know she accepted the apology. "Well, at least you have a niche. Murphy says not having a niche is my niche." She grinned.

Grey dug his heel into the ground like he was thinking it over. Birdie was right. Generally, he did look a little sad.

"Well, see you in a few hours," Leeda said awkwardly, pulling away from the pony and brushing herself off.

She tottered into the house and made her way up to her grandmom's room. She tumbled out of her dirty clothes and crawled under the covers in her skivvies. But she was too wound up to sleep, and she read from one of her grandmother's civil war novels instead.

It was just approaching dawn when she put the book down. The barely gray light outside calmed her.

She was dead tired. But she still couldn't sleep. Maybe it was the end of her eighteen-year animal death streak. Or that she kept thinking about that pony's heartbeat pulsing under her hands. She thought about Grey's face, how different it looked when he actually smiled.

Finally, on a sudden, strong impulse, she got out of bed and pulled her dirty clothes back on, walked downstairs, picked up her keys, and got into her car.

She drove to the ASPCA. The doors were still closed and locked, but Leeda didn't mind waiting. She didn't know what she'd do with the Chihuahua once she had him, if he was still there, but for once, having a plan seemed less important to her than doing something. She hoped she wasn't too late.

Eighteen

Some people can predict whether it's going to rain or sense when something bad is going to happen. Murphy had a sixth sense about people hitting on her. She could see it from a mile away, the way a spider can see the movements of a fly. As she approached the counter of Ganax Heating, she tried to look as uninterested as possible.

"Is Jodee here?" she asked. She stood at the counter, digging her toes into the linoleum floor. The receptionist was a young guy about her age.

"Hey, Murphy." She suddenly recognized him. He'd been in her high school English class. He'd occasionally tracked her down at her locker and had used complex vocabulary words while he talked to her, trying to impress her.

"I had a huge crush on you. You were really smart."

Murphy sighed. She was incredibly bored. "Precognitive, actually."

He blinked at her for a moment. "Yeah, you were really good in English."

Murphy's usage of SAT-level vocabulary usually halted the

moment she got out of class. She had a thing against big words. In her view, they were superfluous. And she hated the word *superfluous.*

"I don't like being liked for my brain," she said. The guy looked befuddled.

"Hey, honey." Her mom suddenly appeared wearing a gray skirt and jacket, slightly too big for her, with a red blouse underneath. "We're in the lunchroom. Come on back."

Murphy followed her mom through the gray-carpeted, fluorescent-lit halls of Ganax, winding back to the small, rectangular lunchroom. Her mom smiled back at her cheerfully and handed her a Snickers bar from her lunch bag. Murphy wondered how someone with so many secrets could look her in the eye so innocently.

They sat down at the table near her mom's coworkers. Murphy had known these women for ages—Lorraine, Carla, and Sandee. She apparently had arrived in the middle of a story, because Lorraine asked, "So what did the people at T-Mobile say?"

"They said they'd be willing to refund me half of the bill," Carla said. "I was like, 'That's fine that you want to give me half, but what about the other half?' And they said they were sorry, but there was nothing they could do about the other half, and that even though the name of the plan said it was unlimited, it wasn't actually unlimited. . . ."

Murphy looked at the other women, including her mother, who were all nodding sympathetically. She couldn't imagine living this life and hearing about this stuff. Did her mom feel obligated to act like the cell phone story was interesting? Couldn't she just tell Carla that the story made her want to burst her own eardrums? Conversations like this were like a living death.

"What brings you here, Murphy?" Lorraine asked.

Murphy had calculated it all. Arrive at lunchtime. Be surrounded by others.

"I want my mom to tell me who my dad is."

Jodee choked on her chicken-salad sandwich. Lorraine looked like a bird that'd just flown into a window—dazed. Carla and Sandee shifted awkwardly.

Murphy knew she was humiliating her mom. But she didn't feel any remorse.

"Murphy, that's inappropriate," Jodee said, but without much strength.

"I deserve to know. Don't you think I deserve to know?" she asked the three other women rhetorically. She turned to her mom. "I saw you at the courthouse. You and my dad and Judge Abbott."

Jodee looked completely bewildered.

"Murphy, why are you trying to embarrass me like this?"

"Why are you trying to embarrass me?" Murphy demanded. "Don't you think it's embarrassing to find out your exboyfriend's sneaking over to your house to see your mom?"

Jodee's face cracked. Murphy knew how the accusation sounded in front of all her friends. She hadn't meant it to come out that way. But she kept plowing forward.

"Why was Rex at our house?"

"I'm gonna go," Carla said. The other women stood up to follow her, and they all trickled out the door with a tangible sense of relief.

Jodee carefully folded the plastic wrap of her sandwich into smaller and smaller squares. "Rex has been helping me with some things."

"Behind my back?"

"There are just some things. . . . I just needed help, and Rex has been there."

Murphy kicked back her chair, furious. "He didn't even tell me he was in town, but he's there for you?"

"Murphy," Jodee said sternly. "Being there for me *is* being there for you. It's helping at a distance."

This boggled Murphy's mind. She didn't know how to respond to it.

"Why at a distance? What does that mean?"

"Well, maybe Rex wants what's best for you, but he can't be around you." The plastic wrap had been folded into the smallest square possible. If her mom folded it any more, it would become an atom.

"That's such a cop-out," Murphy said, feeling her features harden with bitter disdain.

"Murphy." Jodee stood up. "That boy would have done anything for you." She threw her lunch into the garbage can, and Murphy felt the unbearable, infuriating helplessness of being walked away from. "I can't say you would have done the same for him."

Murphy couldn't find a reply. She had expected a mom who was guilty, sorry, and ready to give her what she wanted. But Jodee looked composed, angry, and strong. Murphy clenched and unclenched her fists, staring at her palms. She had expected to walk away with something big and necessary. Now it felt like she was moving a step backward. "What are you trying to say?" she asked.

Jodee tilted her head, studying her sadly, as if she felt bad for her. "Oh, Murphy, I'm saying you want what pleases you, and you won't stand anything that doesn't. And that's why you miss everything important." And then she pushed her way out into the hall.

One night, years after that summer, Emma Ruiz woke in her own bedroom in Mexico to a strange fluttering. She thought it was her own heart. But when she rose and walked to the window, she saw it was the moonlight itself that was fluttering, dropping light through the trees like tiny white petals. It struck a memory in her of something that she had lost and never grieved for.

Nineteen

*P*oopie and Murphy cooked a big "Get Well Soon" meal for Birdie, full of her favorite things. Orange soda. Lasagna. Lucky Charms. A couple of the women workers were there, as it was an all-girl affair. After they ate, they sat around the circular kitchen table playing poker.

Birdie's bandaged foot was propped up on the chair. Majestic sat on her lap, looking at her as if they were survivors of the same kind of trauma. But Birdie was in a great mood. The sprained ankle was a small obstacle. Over the past few, physically useless days, she had been doing her research. And she felt like she had a handle on her house, the farm, and everything in it. She was, in a word, optimistic.

"It's okay," Birdie was saying. "I can still totally work." She stood up as if to demonstrate, grabbing a big bowl of salad off the kitchen counter and carrying it to the table. "I hardly ever use my left leg anyway. I mean, I use it. But for kicking and things like that, I use my right."

"Birdie." Poopie frowned. "The doctor said you need to take it easy for three or four weeks." She slid three more Cheerios, which they were using as poker chips, into the center of the table.

"It's only really the one foot I have to be off of," Birdie said brightly.

Poopie shot a beleaguered look at Murphy that was not lost on Birdie. Murphy looked back helplessly.

Birdie, distracted, hobbled around the room like a carpenter sizing things up. Leeda kept having to remind her when it was her turn, and she'd come back and shove some Cheerios into the pile, always the wrong number. "I fold," she said.

"Then why are you betting?" Murphy asked, putting her hand against her forehead and shaking her head.

Birdie stared at the table. "Oh." She pulled the Cheerios back. It had been like this the whole game.

"Anyway, I've always been good at handy stuff. Ever heard of joists? I read that I can put joists under the whole ground floor."

She walked to a particularly saggy area and tapped it hard with her crutch for emphasis. There was a crunching underneath her. Birdie's eyes widened. And then, with a loud ripping sound, the floor simply gave way beneath her and she went plummeting downward. Murphy lunged, but it was too late. Birdie was waist-deep in the hole, with only her hands and arms holding her from sinking deeper.

Pain seared up her leg. "Oh my God, I think I resprained my sprain."

It took all of them to drag her out. A waft of cavelike, musty odors followed her in. Leaning against the counter, they all breathed heavily. "Are you okay?"

Birdie nodded, unsure, the pain subsiding. She rubbed her

knee, which had gotten scraped, and peered at the hole in the floor.

A sound separated itself from the chaos of them talking. It was a tapping on the glass of the window behind them.

They all looked up and around at the same time.

A face was staring at them. Or staring, more specifically, at Murphy.

Murphy froze like the Hamburglar caught with a plate of burgers. Then she turned to Birdie, as if Birdie would know what to do. But before she could respond, Murphy had composed herself, turned, and walked up the stairs. Even though they had just locked eyes, she pretended she hadn't seen Rex at all.

Murphy was safely in Birdie's room when she heard them letting Rex in through the front door. She cursed Birdie's bedroom door for not having a lock and focused on the window, peering out at the overgrown garden. Could she climb out on the lattice?

Immediately she knew it was out of the question. The sad thing was that Rex would probably look for her there. She ducked into the closet instead, hiding behind some of Birdie's old coats and leaving the door open to throw him off.

She heard two sets of footsteps come into the room, one making more of a limp thudding sound. "Murphy?" Birdie said. "Rex is here to see you."

Both sets of footsteps came directly to the closet. Rex moved the coats aside and stared in at her.

Then Birdie got an embarrassed look on her face, like she wasn't supposed to be there, and disappeared.

Rex and Murphy stood for a second, staring at each other. Rex was a full seven inches taller, with a comfortable slouch and an amused half smile he never seemed to lose. But he looked older than she remembered, more filled out. More grown up. Murphy stared at him, humiliated. But there was his smile. And it was hard to look back at him without an unwelcome grin creeping onto her lips.

"Did you think I was a scary monster?" he asked.

"No."

"You wanna go somewhere? Hang out for a little? We could go to Waffle House."

Murphy stepped out of the closet. "What are you doing here?"

Rex stuck his hands in his pockets and just looked at her like the answer was obvious. Murphy's eyes were stuck to him like magnets. It was like spotting a part of herself she hadn't seen in a while. Something that had been her other half.

"I don't really feel like it," she said.

Rex smiled gently, clearly a little hurt. "Murphy, can't we just catch up? Don't make me beg. Not in front of—" He nodded to Majestic, who was sitting in the doorway watching them, head cocked to the side, giant ears up and alert.

Murphy sighed, letting Rex grab her fingers and pull her away from the closet. She sat on the box spring of the bed, empty of a mattress thanks to Birdie.

"It's stuffy in here," Murphy said lamely, disgruntled.

Rex opened wide one of Birdie's windows and let in the night air from above the garden. He sat next to her on the bed.

Rex rolled his hands together into one fist, thoughtful. They sat awkwardly for a few moments.

"So how's New York? Are you happy? Is it what you thought it would be?"

Murphy blinked at him. "Yeah. It's great. I love it."

Rex nodded encouragingly. "That's good, Shorts. I'm really happy for you." Murphy hated the encouraging nods. It made her feel petty that she couldn't give him the same good wishes.

"I could never go back," Murphy said. "You know, to answering to people like you have to do in Bridgewater. New York's anonymous. It's free."

It was like they were speaking in code. And Murphy was trying to say, in every way she could, that she didn't need him or long for him. They were sitting inches apart, and to her, it could have been miles. It felt like cold metal in her stomach that they were so far away from each other now.

"What's up with you?" she asked.

"I started making furniture. Out of recycled wood and stuff like that. I'm gonna sell some at this art shop in Austin, once we're settled out there. We had an offer on the house we had to take, so we're just living in the hotel till we're ready to go."

"That's great, Rex." Rex always had been gifted with his hands. Murphy didn't want to think about his hands, though.

"I think Austin will be cool. I guess. You know I didn't want to move to a city."

Murphy knew. Rex hadn't come with her to New York for just that reason. And now he was moving to a city anyway. It wasn't lost on her.

Murphy felt like Rex secretly being at her mom's was hanging between them, but she was unwilling to broach it. It felt too intimate.

They got quiet. Murphy couldn't think of a single thing more she had to say to him. Apparently neither could he. Was this how it worked? You loved someone, and then you couldn't manage a five-minute conversation with them? Murphy's gut throbbed with hurt.

"Well," she said, stretching as if she were tired and relaxed. Inside, her chest felt icy and her mouth had gone dry. "I guess I'll call you."

"Yeah." He sighed. "It'll be hard without my number, though." He took a pen off Birdie's dresser and wrote it on her hand on the web between the thumb and the forefinger. "I'll hold my breath, of course." He grinned wryly.

Murphy shrugged as if it were no big thing either way. He glanced at her reluctantly, and then stood up. He looked like he was going to say more, but he just shoved his hands in his pockets, turned, and left. Murphy listened to his truck start up outside and pull away. An image popped into her mind of when they used to lie on his couch in the dark. How close he was and how much it felt like their bodies weren't there at all, and it was just something deeper in both of them that was touching.

In New York, she had met passionate people, creative people, interesting people. But she had never met anyone like Rex.

Murphy had never longed for her dad. Maybe it was all the paternity stuff, but oddly, she longed for him now. She longed to talk to someone who could tell her she had done the right things, let go of the right things, like he had. Someone who could tell her that giving people up was worth it if in the end it meant you were being true to yourself.

But who she was being true to by letting Rex go, she didn't quite know.

Eliza Finkle, the mail mistress, was on her way to the ASPCA on Tuesday afternoon to drop off a litter of kittens her cat had recently delivered when she stopped because of a strange popping sound right in front of Darlington Orchard. She got out to check the wheels and found that a jaggedly sharp rock she'd run over had punctured her tire. While she waited for AAA, it occurred to her that she might as well drop the cats off at the miniature pony rescue instead, the one that old mule Eugenie Cawley-Smith had started. It was closer. Whatever they decided to do with the kittens was their business. It was out of her hands.

Twenty

It started with Leeda coming for a couple afternoons here and there. She would hover over Grey's shoulder to learn a few of the things she didn't know, and to do some minor things she knew how to do on her own, like feeding the ponies, or tidying up the tack room, or simply sitting with the Chihuahua for a while, giving him attention.

Twice, she had shown up to the cottage to find animals left on the front porch. Once a box of kittens, curled up against each other in a knot, sleeping, and then another dog, this time a hunting dog, so skinny she could count his ribs.

Now Leeda skipped up to the house. She had even started to look forward to seeing the ponies, though she still felt like most of them were strangers. She felt triumphant about Sneezy.

As she opened the door, the Chihuahua came running to greet her like they were being reunited after years torn apart, bouncing like a pogo stick. Leeda tried to keep him at arm's length, but he shot out his tongue at her palms, kissing her frantically. She grimaced.

The ancient radio by the kitchen door was blaring punk rock.

Leeda doubted Grandmom's radio had been played loudly a day in her life. Grey emerged from his bedroom, his shirt off and a bunch of shaving cream on his face, his razor poised in midair. When he saw her, his eyes widened and he quickened his pace toward the radio, turning it down, then turned and disappeared into his bedroom. Leeda hesitated in the doorway, suddenly uncomfortable. She listened to the sound of the sink running.

The Chihuahua continued to fling himself against Leeda's shins. Finally she picked him up gingerly and tucked him into her arms, cradling him. She had discovered, the last time she'd come, that he liked to be held like a baby. "You smell bad," she said.

Grey reappeared with a clean face and a dark blue T-shirt on.

"You're so early," he said.

Leeda shrugged. She'd found herself leaving the orchard earlier and earlier to come work with the ponies.

"I haven't eaten breakfast yet," Grey said.

"Me neither."

Grey made some eggs and toast, and then they moved out onto the sunporch, which Grey had taken over, throwing blankets on the formal stiff-backed couch to soften it up and putting candles on the side table so that he could read by it at night. He sank onto the armchair as Leeda dropped her purse by her side and fell back on the couch. They sipped coffee and ate.

For now, they were keeping the hunting dog in a pen out back that Grey had put up, and the kittens were staying in Grey's room until Leeda could figure out what she wanted to do with them. She guessed she'd list them on Petfinder.com as she had the Chihuahua a few days before.

"I've named him," Grey said through a mouthful, gesturing to the Chihuahua, who was curled up possessively beside Leeda on the couch.

"Oh. You know, I can't keep him. It's probably not a good idea to—"

"Mr. Barky Von Schnauzer," Grey interrupted.

Leeda sucked in her bottom lip, gazing at him. "Like from the commercial?"

"Yeah." Grey nodded.

"That's awful."

"That's why it's great." He looked at her, openly pleased with the name. Guys could be so simple and dumb. Eric, for instance, loved wrestling.

Leeda rolled her eyes.

The eggs were delicious. Grey had put a bunch of herbs in and some onions.

"These are good."

"I learned from one of my foster parents."

Leeda nodded. "My mom wouldn't let me in the kitchen," she offered by way of being a little open too. It seemed only right. "She said I'd mess it up. The cook was the only one allowed."

Finally they finished their food, and Leeda moved to get up, knocking her bag off the couch. It went tumbling forward, and its contents came falling out.

Grey leaned forward, analyzing what was on the floor: a pepper shaker shaped like a little Airstream trailer. Half of an old crayon. A screwdriver. And, most telltale of all, a Fabergé egg that had been sitting on her grandmother's shelf until a few days before.

"What is all this stuff?" he asked as she bent down to sweep them up. Barky leaped down in a flash to sniff around and see if any of the fallen objects were food.

Leeda sputtered, mortified. "Just some things . . ."

Grey looked at her, his mouth open in amazement. He reached forward and held up a Miss Piggy figurine, a question on his face. "What are you, a magpie?"

Leeda blushed furiously. She swiped the Miss Piggy out of his hand, hastily scooped up the items, and put them back in her bag.

They both stood, looking at each other.

"What's all that for?" he asked.

Leeda could easily have refused to answer the question. She didn't know why she felt the urge to tell him. She didn't know him.

"I take them. From places. I just . . . started . . . when I got home this summer. It's usually nothing important. I guess the Fabergé egg is, but that's not why I took it."

"So why?" Grey asked.

Leeda shrugged. "I don't know." She looked at the objects. The majority of them were from the orchard. But there were a couple from her grandmom's house too, and some from her parents' house. "To remind me."

A soft, surprised smile played about Grey's lips. Like she suddenly was someone different to him than he'd thought she was. "Of what?"

Leeda felt how stupid it sounded. "I don't know. Where I'm from."

"You're from Sesame Street?" he demanded lustily, thrusting Miss Piggy into the air again.

Leeda felt a smirk creeping onto her face to match his. It was a moment of understanding between them. It was real, and it was ridiculous.

"It's just . . ." She swallowed. "This stuff reminds me that I've had a life no one else has had. That I'm not . . . this default person."

Grey's smile was gone. He was staring at her intently. She wondered if maybe it was insensitive to talk about how much she needed to remember where she was from, when he wasn't from anywhere.

"Hello?"

At the sound of the voice, they both turned, stood, and walked out into the parlor. The front door was open, and Birdie was just emerging from Grey's room, a kitten cradled in her hand. "Aww, they are so cute," she moaned, beaming at them delightedly and rubbing the kitten up against her face.

"Hey, Birdie, how's the leg?" Grey asked, turning his eyes from Leeda to her.

"Um. Good," Birdie said, blushing. They hadn't seen each other since she'd landed on him. Leeda marveled at how familiar she already was with the kitten.

Birdie cradled the kitten to her chest and looked at Barky, who was standing at Leeda's right heel, staring at Birdie with a removed gaze, sizing her up like she was a guest.

"I thought you gave him to someone," she said.

"I went and got him back," Leeda said. "The other ones are just piling up."

"I think Barky sent out a message in a bottle to all the other strays," Grey added, giving Leeda a look. "Is that the way of it, Barky?" he asked like a detective, staring down at the dog.

Barky looked completely content, rolling his eyes up to Leeda trustingly and occasionally licking his nervous little lips, then rolling them toward Birdie, as if to make sure she wasn't going to ruin the moment by stealing Leeda away.

"Can I name one of the kittens Captain Catpants?" Birdie gushed excitedly.

Leeda laughed. "Yeah, Bird, whatever you want. You can name all of them."

Birdie moved up and down on her toes a little, grinning. And then she turned serious. "You should make sure you get them all spayed or neutered," she said. "You could probably work out a discount with a vet."

"So what have you been up to, Birdie, besides falling on innocent bystanders?" Grey asked. It was strange how immediately easy he was with Birdie. Birdie, even though she was shy, had that way with people. Leeda admired and envied it.

Birdie smiled. "I'm trying to keep my house," she said. "Actually," she added as if she were just remembering something, "that's why I'm here." She looked at Leeda. "I came to see if you wanted to come to Southern Counties with me. I need to buy some supplies. For the house."

"Oh, Bird, I can't. I have so much going on, and I haven't talked to Eric in three days. He's gonna forget me," she joked. "Can I help tomorrow?"

Birdie stuck her hands in the pockets of her overalls. "Sure."

"I'll go with you," Grey offered.

Leeda and Birdie both looked at him, surprised.

"I'm really handy. And I could use a change of scenery."

"Well . . . I really could use the help. If you don't mind," Birdie said.

Leeda suddenly felt left behind. She watched Grey disappear into his room and come out a moment later with his keys. In another moment, he and Birdie were heading out the door.

Leeda walked up to the window, watching them go. She couldn't put her finger on the sense of loss she had. It was probably just the fact that the cottage was suddenly quiet.

But then again, not really. Barky was at her heels, and he let out a low, plaintive growl. She scooped him up and held him to her face the way Birdie had held the kitten—so naturally. They sniffed each other's noses.

It felt kind of good.

Twenty-one

Almost everyone was at church, so the orchard was deserted when Birdie and Grey pulled in. They climbed out of the truck, and Birdie hobbled around to the back, which was full of sacks of sand, mortar, a trowel, and a big red bucket. Birdie wasn't sure what she would use yet, but she could take back the things she didn't.

"So how're you going to do this, Birdie?" Grey asked as he grabbed a couple of bags and Birdie led the way across the grass.

"Well, the house has been settling because of the soft ground. You know, with the caves underneath. But if I can move some concrete pilings and cylinders in there and position them across the soft bits, it will stabilize the bottom of the foundation." They were rounding the side of the house and heading back into the shade.

Grey looked impressed but skeptical. "But Birdie, for something like that, you need to be able to load the pilings in, because they're huge and heavy...."

Birdie halted when they were just under the kitchen window. "I'm gonna hire someone to do that. Just the unloading," she answered. "And then I can roll them in on a low dolly." She laid her crutches down on the grass. Through the crawl space here, they could get in to right under where Birdie had fallen through the floor.

"And you need to be able to maneuver well underneath."

"Yeah," Birdie said. "I don't have to get a hydraulic jack. But you can rent them. And they're not that expensive."

Grey shook his head at her and laughed. "My mistake. I thought you were just your everyday amateur." His voice was deep and sounded soothing to Birdie. She studied the dirt caked under his fingernails. She didn't see how Leeda thought he was so bad. He seemed really nice to her. But Birdie usually got along with people. She knew she was pretty unintimidating.

She glanced around. From this side of the house—the opposite side from Murphy's garden and Birdie's bedroom window—the farm sloped off, away from the peach trees and up toward the northwestern corner, which was just grass and scattered trees and a gradual rise to the edge of the property. There it butted against a back road that wound down to meet Orchard Road. It was an inviting area, probably because it was so remote and unvisited. It just sat still.

It was things like this—the old, musty smell coming out from the crawl space and the shade on the grass—that gave Birdie moments of extreme, aching love for her home.

"So Leeda's your cousin, huh?" Grey asked.

"Second cousin."

"Have you always gotten along?"

Birdie pulled on a long-sleeve shirt that she'd tied around her waist. "I didn't know her, I mean, *really* know her, for a long time.

I always thought she was all perfect and kind of conceited. But she's just reserved. And not so perfect." Birdie stopped short then waved her hands, worried that Grey would think she meant something negative. "In a good way. You know, like a human.

"I'm sorry you guys don't get along," she added, flustered. She knelt down, unloading a flashlight from another bag she'd brought.

"Leeda said we don't get along?" Grey asked, turning serious and awkwardly focused.

"Oh." Birdie bit her lip as she looked up at him, mortified. "No. Uh, I don't know."

They were both silent for a moment, Birdie checking to make sure the batteries worked in the flashlight, her knees sinking into the soft grass.

"Do you like her boyfriend?" Grey asked.

Birdie blinked up at him. "Never met him," she said. "She's crazy about him, though. He must be pretty great. Because Leeda's not the type to just be crazy about anyone. She kind of holds back." She leaned forward onto her elbows, and Grey came to stand next to her as she peered into the darkness under the house. "I need to get down there and see what it looks like. And then I'll start measuring everything," she said.

"You can't shimmy under the house with a sprained ankle, Birdie."

"It's not a big deal."

"All right." He looked pained. "I'll come too. I'll hold the flashlight."

"You don't have to."

Grey flashed her a game smile and clicked the flashlight on.

His teeth were white against his tanned face and the faint but dark stubble dusting his chin. He had stunning eyes. Birdie was temporarily caught off guard by them.

"Okay." Birdie got down on her knees and then leaned forward on her elbows, squishing down and half-crawling, half-shimmying into the darkness under the house. Grey followed. She could hear him behind her, the sound of his knees moving first on grass, then on dirt. The beam of the flashlight bounced along in front of her.

Birdie could make out the sagging slats of the house in the dimness. Grey crawled up beside her, and they made their way a little further up to the place where the light came in through the hole in the floor above them. Birdie shimmied a little bit more to get a better look. Suddenly, as she moved her hands forward, she felt nothing beneath them, and she jerked back just in time to bump into Grey.

"Watch out," she said, and her voice echoed weirdly. Grey sidled up next to her.

They were at the edge of a gaping hole.

Birdie ran her hands along the edge, feeling it like someone blind might feel a face. A musty air rose from the dark and cooled her cheeks.

It was too dark to see very much, but the cave gave off a feeling of hugeness and emptiness. And at the same time, it didn't seem quite empty of beauty. Birdie felt like she was peering into the beating heart underneath her home. She looked up at the bottom of the house. As her eyes adjusted, she could see the places where the foundation was buckling in.

Birdie was speechless. But she couldn't move. She was mesmerized to think that the cave had sat gaping under her house her whole life. And that it had been here, probably, for millions of years, long before the house existed. And that it would be here long after the house was gone.

They were silent for a few seconds, and then Grey finally spoke softly. "Birdie, there's no way you can fix this." She heard him start to back up.

Dazed, she followed him, crawling backward.

They emerged into the sun again, covered in dust. Birdie took deep breaths, relieved to be back out in the open. She looked at Grey, unsure what she wanted to communicate but sure that it was huge and that she was powerless.

But Grey seemed to recognize fear when he saw it. And he simply reached forward and pulled Birdie to him.

She sank against his chest. It felt different than Enrico's body. Taller and firmer. It felt safe.

Twenty-two

$\mathcal{M}$urphy lay in bed, staring at the ceiling.

It had been a typical night of sitting in the common room with the other women, gossiping and watching movies, fanning themselves with newspapers, the windows propped wide open for air. In some places, Murphy knew, the night air in the summer got much cooler and fresher. But in southern Georgia, it stayed warm all night. In her trailer, which didn't have AC, the heat had always kept Murphy awake, sweating and longing for the summers she knew they were having in Maine or northern California.

Now she lay on top of her sheets with the regulation flannel blankets the Darlingtons gave for each bed lying in a knot on the floor beside her. She hadn't felt so restless and hemmed in since before she'd left for New York. It was like old ghosts had come back to haunt her. The ghosts of too small, not enough.

Finally Murphy slid out from under the covers. She glanced over at Leeda's empty bed. For the past couple of nights, Leeda had slept at Primrose Cottage. Apparently an injured ferret had arrived, and Leeda was too worried to leave it alone at night.

Murphy opened her door slowly and tiptoed down the hall, pulling her long tank top down over her flimsy boxers. In another couple of moments she was outside, padding barefoot down the wooden stairs. The crickets were deafening. The peach trees were shadows.

She walked across the moonlit grass and climbed the ladder to Birdie's tree house, her soles wet from the grass. She paused on the top rung.

Birdie was peacefully asleep, curled up under an old quilt, a night-light beside her. Murphy rethought and climbed back down, jumping off the second-to-last rung onto the grass. She returned to the dorms and got a couple of quarters and a crumpled piece of paper with a phone number on it from her dresser. She pulled on jeans over her boxers, slipped a bra on under her tank top, and stepped into her flip-flops. Then she headed over to the barn and got on the pay phone.

A sleepy voice answered.

"Hey, can we go somewhere?"

Rex was there ten minutes later.

"Where we going?" He yawned, seeming to become more alert as they pulled out and drove.

"It's off exit seventeen."

The parking lot of Buckets was practically empty. It was a Wednesday night. Murphy climbed out of the car and, reluctantly, Rex followed her.

They walked in and sank onto two stools near the bar. A woman with curly ash-colored hair sat at the corner of the bar, playing a little electronic trivia game. Murphy ordered a beer for herself and smiled smugly at Rex when she wasn't carded. Rex rolled his eyes and ordered a milk.

While they waited for their drinks, Murphy kicked the leg of the table with her dangling toes, and Rex looked at her expectantly, clearly wanting to know why they were there.

But Murphy was coy. "What?" she asked, grinning.

He caught one of her feet between his own. "Be real with me, Murphy. Why are we here?"

Murphy shrugged. "I dunno. I thought it would be fun." She figured that he hadn't been real with her either.

Rex stood up and dug three twenties out of his wallet. "Here's cab money." He gave her a pained look. "Be safe getting home." He turned to leave. Murphy knew he would too.

"Wait. I'm sorry." She stood up and pulled Rex back by the sleeve. "Rex, I'm sorry."

He turned to her. "Murphy, I can tell when you're trying to cajole someone into doing things your way. But this is me. I know you."

The waitress arrived carrying their drinks.

To Murphy's relief, they both sat back down, looking at each other as the beer and the milk were set on the table. Then Murphy glanced up at the waitress unsurely. "Do you know a guy who comes in here, green eyes, mustache?" she said.

"Sorry, honey." She walked away.

Rex was staring at her questioningly.

Murphy took a sip of her drink. "My mom found my dad. But she won't tell me who he is or anything about him. I thought he might be here because I followed him here before."

"How do you know it was your dad?" Rex seemed bewildered.

"I know it's him. I saw him coming out of the courthouse with her."

Rex absorbed this solemnly for a moment. "Murphy, maybe your mom has reasons for not telling you. Maybe she's protecting you."

Murphy balked. "Protecting me from what? From not knowing my genetic makeup? What if I'm prone to female-pattern baldness or something?"

"Maybe she doesn't think having a dad in your life all of a sudden would be a good thing."

Murphy stared at him, trying to stare into him, suspicious.

"She's probably just worried he'll hurt my feelings," she said with forced carelessness. "By not being interested. But seriously, I don't care."

They sat a while longer, and Rex seemed to become increasingly impatient. "Murph, why are we here? I mean, really here?"

Murphy didn't know how to answer that question. She knew the likelihood of her dad just happening to be there was slim. All she knew was that he'd come here once.

Rex got up to go to the bathroom. Murphy leaned on her elbows, listless, staring around the bar. Finally she stood and walked over to the wall and studied the photos hanging there.

It was full of pictures of people who'd spent time at the bar—the family of the bar owners, babies even, and a grainy photo of the original owner in 1973.

It was like looking at history. These were people who'd stayed in one place all their lives—the opposite of Murphy.

Maybe it was a thread she was looking for. Just a tiny thread between her and her father.

She trailed back to the bar. Rex had returned and was sitting there on the stool watching her, looking worried.

"We can go," she said.

On the way back, they were quiet. But it wasn't a bad silence.

Murphy studied him out of the corner of her eye from time to time. It was 2 a.m. before they were back at the foot of the driveway. "You can just leave me here," she said.

"Are you gonna call me again?" he asked.

"I don't know."

She hopped down onto the gravel and closed the door behind her, giving Rex a wave through the window. It hurt to watch him pull away without a promise she'd see him again. But Murphy didn't want to be depended on.

Maybe that was another thing she and her dad had in common.

Twenty-three

Rooooooooo.

It was midafternoon and sweltering. Leeda had locked up Barky in his crate because it was Baxter the hunting dog's time to play in the house. Barky and Baxter didn't get along, mostly because Barky was jealous of Baxter. Barky was very possessive of Leeda, like a firstborn, and he didn't like to share her. Over the weeks, he had weaseled his way into being Leeda's bedmate whenever she stayed at the cottage, mostly because he wouldn't stop crying and yelping till she went downstairs, got him, and pulled him into her bed. It had been difficult for her, sleeping with a dog. Getting his fur all over the sheets, having her face licked in the morning, listening to his snoring. But, slowly, she had gotten used to it.

Now she went up to his crate and gave him a stern look that quieted him down. He looked at her guiltily. But she knew as soon as she turned around, he'd start yelping again.

Still, Leeda was in a good mood. Even though, despite countless Internet searches and phone calls, she hadn't found anyone willing to take the ponies—not even one of them. The fact was, she felt confident. She felt as though, for the first time in her life, she were doing something good for the world.

Exhausted, she looked at the clock. Almost noon and she was way behind. She headed out to the barn lot, swiped back her sweaty hair, and began pouring feed into all the buckets. She didn't know how Grey had ever done it all alone. It was hard enough for her to share it with him fifty-fifty, and he did all the heavier, more difficult work.

The ponies were in high spirits, racing each other around the field. They moved like a clutch of bees, all turning and weaving as if on some secret signal. When they tired and stopped running, they milled around, watching Leeda or playing with one another.

Sneezy had taken a special interest in Leeda and often walked over to spend time with her while the rest of the ponies socialized. The pony would follow her around, watching Leeda curiously as she swept out the stalls or spread fresh straw. Leeda didn't welcome her, but she didn't shoo her away either.

The Baron was much more mischievous. He would come by and nip Leeda on her butt or tug at the hem of her shirt, and then, when she whipped around, he'd run back to the other ponies. Sometimes she could swear they all seemed to be snickering. And that they liked Grey best. They nuzzled up to him and let him pet them and never nipped him.

In any case, the nips hurt. Leeda found bruises in the mirror when she undressed at night.

She and Grey spent much of each day not talking, just focusing on their tasks, but when they crossed paths they smiled or nodded at each other. At mealtimes they sat on the sunporch with the windows open and rested. Sometimes Grey would read for twenty minutes or so after eating, and Leeda would just stare out at the barn lot, content to sit in silence.

Between the ponies and the animals (the grand total of strays was now ten) and trying to get to the orchard whenever she could, Leeda felt she never had a second to herself anymore. She was thinking about this as she poured feed into the last of the pony troughs. Hearing footsteps behind her, she turned to see Grey.

He looked sweaty and tired, his T-shirt pasted against him and a film of dust covering his long, lean arms.

"Where do you want me to build the new pen?" he asked. Leeda thought. They had already built two pens for the dogs to run in, but now Leeda wanted to give the bunnies—there were two—some room too.

"I guess we could do them along the wall," Leeda said. "So there's shade." She had gotten a little handy over the past couple weeks and had learned how to nail pens together and stretch chicken wire over the wooden frames. She still didn't know what she'd do with the animals when she left. She never had time to step back and figure out what her plan was. She was merely reacting.

Leeda leaned against the wall of the stall. "Phew," she said. August was just around the corner. "It has to cool down soon, doesn't it?"

Grey studied her for a moment. "Why don't we get out of here for a while?"

"Now?" Leeda looked up toward the house, thinking of all the stuff she had to do up there once she was done with the barn lot.

"Oh God, I don't have time. I've got to get online once we're done and—"

Grey reached out and took her elbow, smiling, amused. "C'mon, Leeda."

She let him drag her out onto the porch, and then down to the front of his truck. He pulled her around to the passenger side and opened the door. Then he lifted her up roughly, like a wet fish, and dumped her onto the seat. Leeda rubbed her elbows where he'd picked her up, even though they didn't hurt.

He drove in the opposite direction of town, down a winding back road that seemed to go on forever. Leeda was too tired to ask where they were going and too bleary-eyed to follow the scenery.

"So what are you gonna do with all that money?" Grey asked after about ten minutes, his hands confident and lazy on the wheel.

Leeda flopped her head to look in his direction, resting her neck on the top of the backrest. "Shop." She smiled, half-joking.

Grey nodded.

"You think I'm selfish," Leeda said, wiping away her hair where it was blowing in her eyes and looking back out the window, not really offended. Not really caring.

"Hey, I'm no saint. I don't know what you are. I'd probably buy a ridiculous Italian motorcycle or something. But . . ." He trailed off.

"What?" She looked at him.

"But maybe I'd give it all away and live in a cabin and have everything I needed," he said.

He looked at her, and Leeda didn't know why, but she laughed.

She hadn't asked him when exactly he was leaving for Alaska. She had been scared to. She didn't know how she was going to take care of everything without him.

"I'd buy something I'd get tired of," she admitted. "I'm fickle."

"Eugenie must have thought more highly of you than that."

Leeda shrugged. "Grandmom contained multitudes, I guess."

"You know what I've been thinking, Leeda?"

She turned to him. "What?"

"You know how you say you're so unsure of what you want and what you like, all that?"

"Yeah." Leeda felt slightly embarrassed. And she wondered where he was headed.

"I was just thinking, maybe that's not such a bad thing." He glanced over at her. "Maybe figuring it out is . . . I don't know, what it's all about. Constantly deciding. And you're true enough not to decide anything before you're ready, and you don't want to lock yourself into a box. Maybe it's the sure people who are missing out."

The words fell on Leeda heavy as stones. Each one of them hit her somewhere inside, like something she'd never thought of before. A little something in her shook. She didn't say anything. Grey only gave her a half smile and kept driving.

A few minutes later, he slowed down and parked at a small makeshift parking spot nestled into the side of the road among the trees. Leeda followed him into the thin swath of woods. They emerged almost immediately onto a long winding creek. Mertie Creek was miles long and ran all through the county.

The water, moving gently, glistened in the sun, winding its way south. It was wide here, and the current was slow. It looked deep, with no rocks poking out, and a rope swing dangled from one of the oak trees overhanging the water.

Grey took off his shirt. He was sunburned on the back of his neck from working in the sun. Leeda felt awkward and stared at the water. "Well, in you go."

Leeda grinned dubiously. "That's a creek. It's way too cold."

Grey studied her, shrugged, and turned, taking a running start into the water. He leaped up for the rope swing and grabbed it, pulling it to the shore with him. Then he proceeded to use it, doing dives and flips. . . .

He was graceful in the water. She'd never seen him look so unfettered. He moved like a different person than the one she'd met in the barn lot at the beginning of the summer.

Leeda finally walked to the water's edge, dipped a toe in, and then started to wade in, first to where the water met the edges of her khaki shorts, then, gasping with the cold, to the bottom of her tank top. Finally, with a kind of surrender, she let herself sink all the way in.

They swam and kicked and splashed.

Grey knelt so Leeda could climb up on the shelf of his thigh to grab the rope. He steadied her by the waist as she reached up for it, stretching herself out of the water. She had to stand on her tiptoes to try and reach it, lower herself, and try again. Within a few seconds her body was covered in goose bumps. Grey's left hand was on her calf.

"What happened?" he asked, reaching out his finger to a spot just above the back of her knee where The Baron had nipped her.

"Ponies," she said, stiffening until his hand went back to her calf.

When she got it, she held the rope like a trophy.

The first time she swung she slid off the rope almost immediately, hitting the water with her feet and letting go. The second time she lifted her knees up, pulled herself into a ball, and gripped. By the third time, she could make it clear to the end of the swing before letting herself drop. Leeda had always been a quick learner.

They roughhoused for a while, splashing each other, and then they got tired. They drifted off to their own areas of the water, Leeda floating on her back and Grey examining some moss at the bank.

Finally she got bored and ducked under the water, swimming toward him, sneaking. She came up right behind him. But either he was pretending he didn't hear her, or he was too absorbed in what he was studying, because he didn't turn around when she popped out of the water. Hesitating and wondering what to do, Leeda froze. She stood a bit too long to do anything. She stared at his back, at his shoulder, at the drops of water on him, at the tilt of his head, feeling curious about whatever was going on in his brain. It was like being hit with an arrow.

She stepped backward, awkwardly, and sank under the water, swimming back toward the shore. She got out and began wringing out her clothes. She waited by the car until he'd come out of the water and dried off with his shirt, putting it back on sopping wet.

On the drive home, they were quiet. Leeda was acutely aware of where every edge of him was. It was like she couldn't be just in her own head.

"I'm gonna wait to go to Alaska. Until you go back to school," he said. "After you've figured everything out."

Leeda felt awkward and grateful. "Thank you," she said.

Grey turned on the radio, and they were silent for the rest of the drive. Leeda wondered if the silence felt as dense and alive to him as it did to her.

A strange car was in the driveway when they pulled in, but Leeda barely registered it.

They both got out of the car a little breathlessly.

At the front of the truck, they stood for a second, smiling at each other with their hands in their pockets. "Thanks, Grey," Leeda said.

"Yeah."

The cottage's front door opened, and Leeda turned, surprised by the sound.

Eric stood in the doorway.

Leeda jumped, yelped with glee, and ran into his arms.

Twenty-four

"I'll have a profiterole," Eric said. Leeda ordered the same. Her mom and dad got the tiramisu and Danay only ordered an espresso.

The Cawley-Smiths were sitting around the table at Abbondanza!, a fancy Italian restaurant in Warner Robbins. It was the nicest place within a sixty-mile radius of Bridgewater, with white tablecloths and candles. They had ridden over in the family car—all four of them—and Danay had driven out from Atlanta to meet them halfway.

Lucretia was gazing at Eric in an approving way that, to Leeda, was almost over the top. Eric kept looking at her sideways, smiling obligingly. Leeda laid her hand against his elbow just to remind him she was there. But he didn't seem to need reassurance. Throughout the dinner, under the stream of questions from her parents about his background, his family, and his interests, his self-confidence had never faltered. Lucretia had conducted the dinner almost like a formal interview. But if Eric had a chink in his armor, it didn't show.

"Did you know Leeda was the Pecan Queen?" Lucretia asked,

fluttering her eyelashes and winking at Leeda. She looked as giddy as a schoolgirl. She had drunk a couple of glasses of wine.

Eric laughed. "What's a Pecan Queen?" His smile was even and perfect. He had worn a soft blue button-down shirt and a gray jacket, and he looked very New York.

"Nothing." Leeda waved her hand.

"Not nothing. It means she's the prettiest girl in town. Her sister was too. And so was her grandmother Eugenie. And so was I." Leeda's father cleared his throat, but Lucretia went on. "Her last boyfriend's dad owned a hardware store," she said, rolling her eyes as if to say weren't they—weren't they three—relieved she'd come to her senses?

"Mom, maybe you should take it easy on the Zinfandel," Danay said, sliding Lucretia's glass out of arm's reach. Leeda shot her a grateful glance, and then looked at Eric contritely, as if to apologize that her mom was a snob and apparently buzzed.

Eric smiled at Leeda, a smile that, between the two of them, said he was not so much horrified as amused. Leeda studied him thoughtfully as his plate was delivered and he placed a bite of profiterole in his mouth. She was undeniably proud of him. But it had been so long since she'd seen him that he felt a little foreign to her. She guessed it was natural. But it wasn't what she'd expected after all the times talking and listening to each other breathe on the phone. She'd expected to feel, when she saw him again, like their souls were entwined or something.

"You look great, Leeda, by the way," he said.

Leeda tossed her head jokingly. "Thanks." But she really did feel like a new girl. She had scrubbed herself silly, even under her fingernails, to get off all the grime from the animals. She had ditched her T-shirt and shorts for a two-hundred-dollar pair of jeans and a silky, jewel-green top. She had seen people looking at her when they'd walked into the restaurant. It felt nice to be looked at by people instead of ponies. Leeda was pretty sure ponies never thought she was pretty.

Her mom patted her hand. "She's going to be a big deal, Eric. Leeda has a bright future ahead of her."

Leeda rolled her eyes, feeling embarrassed. But she was also pleased. She liked to think that her mom thought she would be a big deal. She liked glowing in a silky top at a nice restaurant, with the guy she loved looking at her like she was pure gold. It all seemed clean and clear and lovely. Just the way life should be.

The ride home was jovial, everyone chatting away. Leeda, sitting against the passenger-side window in the back, watched the dark landscape go by, content.

They got out of the car at Breezy Buds, where the Cawley-Smiths had insisted Eric spend the night. It only took a moment for Leeda to notice Grey's car in the driveway. For a split second she felt guilty, as if his being here were a reason for guilt.

Grey was standing on the steps at the front door. Leeda looked at him, perplexed, as they all approached him. Finally they reached him, and they all stood expectantly for a second.

"Grey, these are my parents." Leeda gestured to her mom and dad, her stomach roiling suddenly. "You already met Eric."

"Hey," Grey said, sticking out his hand to shake Leeda's mom's and dad's hands. "Nice to meet you."

They nodded at him politely, gave Leeda a quizzical look, and then walked inside the house. Leeda, Eric, and Grey lingered on the lawn in front of the stairs.

"I just thought you'd want to know," Grey said, his face sober and serious. "Leeda, Barky died."

It was the last thing Leeda expected to hear. She suddenly felt floaty and far away. "What?"

"He just went into this kind of . . . fit. I rushed him to the vet, but he had died by the time we got there. They think he had hepatitis. They said he probably had a fever for a couple days, but we didn't notice. It can happen suddenly, I guess."

A tight pain grabbed onto Leeda's chest and fast tears clouded her vision. "That's not fair," she said disbelievingly. "We took care of him. I . . ."

Leeda stared at Grey, hoping he could somehow fix it. She felt a hand slip into hers and she realized it was Eric's. She'd almost forgotten he was standing there.

"Can you give us a minute?" she asked, turning to him.

Eric studied her face earnestly. "Sure, Lee."

In another moment he'd gone inside, and it was just Leeda and Grey standing and looking at each other. Leeda had the urge to touch him or to give him a hug. But she couldn't bring herself to even say something soothing.

"This stuff happens with animals," Grey said instead, trying to make it sound okay.

"Yeah."

But neither of them thought it was okay. Barky was Barky. Not an animal.

Grey suddenly reached out and pulled her to him in a hug, laying his head on her shoulder. Leeda held the back of his head and hugged him tight, wanting to hold on harder and harder. Instead she pulled back right away.

Feeling awkward and strangely guilty again, she reached out and patted him stiffly on the shoulder. It came out ridiculous and cold. "Well, hang in there," she heard herself saying, sounding like she was coaching baseball.

When she'd gone inside and Grey was gone, she kept looking out the window with a heavy feeling like regret. She didn't know what she regretted. Maybe that she'd taken in Barky at all. Maybe the way she'd patted Grey's shoulder like an acquaintance. Maybe something she hadn't done yet.

Twenty-five

*P*oopie and Birdie sat at the sorting table, sorting peaches. Occasionally one of the workers would come up with a bushel of peaches, dump it, chat with them for a little while in Spanish, and then turn and head back into the trees.

Poopie kept eyeing Birdie sideways, and Birdie knew why. She was giving off darkness in billowing clouds. She was thinking nonstop of the hole under the house, and she was walking around with her head down, lost in thought and scowling in concentration at her shoes, or at peaches, or at whatever else crossed her line of vision. Try as she might, she couldn't work her way around it. And the more she thought of it, the more other observations piled up in her head. The sinking house. Her dad's desire to move on to somewhere new and easier. The money it would take.

Grey had come for the morning to help Walter with an old tractor he was fixing to sell before they moved. Birdie could see him, whenever she looked up, tinkering across the grass.

Next to her, Poopie furiously sorted the peaches, her hands moving so fast it was hard to believe her brain was involved in deciding which peach was perfect, which was damaged enough for cider, and which was somewhere in between and destined for local sale.

"Where will everyone go?" Birdie asked, her hands moving rapidly too, though not as fast as Poopie's. "If we close down?"

"They'll find more work," Poopie said. "They're always looking for more work so they can send money home." She glanced up at Birdie and met her eyes. "They'll scatter." Her brown hands continued to move like butterflies over the bright, round shapes.

Birdie turned to gaze into the peach rows at the occasional worker coming and going. "I can't imagine life without them."

"The best parts of life are the things you can't imagine." Poopie leaned forward to corral some peaches that had gotten away from her.

Birdie tried to imagine the things she couldn't imagine. She slid the last few peaches she was juggling into their proper bins.

"I saw the cave under the house," she finally said.

Poopie's hands halted their movement, as if she were waiting.

Birdie thought about the lines on her dad's face. About how much worry the farm had caused him. And about how it all felt over.

"You guys should sell it," she finally said. She tried to smile at Poopie, tried to be encouraging, but she could feel her lips trembling, giving her away.

Poopie looked at her. She reached over and took her hand. Birdie stared at it for a moment, and then couldn't sit there anymore. She pulled her fingers away and propelled herself toward her crutches.

She ambled past where Grey was working on the tractor and

headed toward the pecan grove. She made it to the fence at the edge of the property and let her crutches drop on the grass. She flung herself against the fence, breathing hard, staring at the end-lessness of the grass in front of her, a giant hole inside her. She could hear the odd pecan falling to the ground from the trees above.

"Birdie." She felt a hand on her shoulder. "Birdie, are you okay?"

Birdie turned to Grey.

She didn't know why he was there. But she reached out for him anyway. She just pulled him to her and then she kissed him.

Twenty-six

Murphy biked circles around the courthouse parking lot like an evil newspaper boy from one of her favorite movies, *Better Off Dead*. She and Judge Miller Abbott didn't have a great history. Since she'd hit puberty, he'd seen her through two shoplifting convictions, countless underage alcohol issues, a few streaking episodes, and the time she'd mutilated the Bob's Big Boy "Big Boy." But Murphy was unfazed. She was going to get him to talk.

When he emerged from the courthouse door at exactly five o'clock, Murphy turned her bike onto its kickstand and climbed off, walking to meet him in the middle of the lot. He looked surprised and a little nervous to see her there.

"Hi, Murphy." He tried to look like it was an average day and an average encounter, but Murphy could tell he guessed why she'd come and it made him nervous. "How are you?" he asked. "How's school?"

"Let's not play games, Judge Abbott," Murphy said, sounding like a forties gangster movie. "You know what I'm here for."

Judge Abbott's usually friendly face went poker blank. "What's that?"

"My dad," she said firmly. "I know you met with him. I was here. I followed him in his LeBaron," she spat. "I need his info. I deserve his info. His name. Address. I have rights."

"Murphy, I—"

"I'm not leaving here without it."

"Murphy, any meetings I have contain confidential information. If your father chooses to reveal his whereabouts . . ."

Over his shoulder, Murphy could see one of the courthouse secretaries walking toward them, presumably to her car.

"I don't know much about bladder-control issues," she said loudly. "But you shouldn't be ashamed to ask the pharmacist—"

"Murphy." The judge looked more disappointed in her than embarrassed. He looked over his shoulder and nodded at the secretary.

"You know, lots of men have that problem," Murphy went on loudly.

But when he turned back to her, she could see it wasn't working. "Murphy," he said solemnly. The tone of his voice arrested her. Murphy looked at him expectantly. "Murphy, that man we met with wasn't your father."

Murphy didn't say anything.

"He was a lawyer. Handling your paternity case. That's all I'm allowed to tell you."

"Allowed by whom?"

"If you don't believe me, we can ask . . ." He gestured in the direction of the secretary getting in her car.

Murphy felt something collapse inside. She looked down at her shoes. "I believe you." When she looked back up, the judge's poker face was gone and had been replaced by an expression of warmth and sympathy.

He reached for her shoulder and patted it. "I'm sorry."

"Don't be sorry. If you're sorry, change it. Say something. Tell me the truth."

Judge Abbott looked thoughtfully at her, long and hard. "I can't. I really am sorry."

"Sorry is for chumps," she said. "You're just a chump."

She didn't wait to see how he took that one. Murphy got on her bike and pedaled away.

It was just dusk at the orchard. Murphy swung left into the drive and slowed her bike, noticing the warm yellow light pouring out of the barn across the grass and the sound of jazzy, old-time music drifting out through the open doors.

She laid her bike against one of the huge oak trees that stood beside the driveway and walked across the grass, curious.

Rex was sitting at the old workbench against the wall, repairing a circular piece of wood. It looked like the top of a banister. He looked up, saw Murphy, and turned back to what he was doing. Probably repairing little things for Walter, Murphy decided. He had been doing odd jobs at the orchard for even longer than Murphy had known Birdie.

Murphy sank down beside him on a stool. The vinyl of the seat cushion was torn, and she could feel the rip through her jeans. It was stuffy in here; outside was much cooler.

She had calmed a bit on her ride home from the courthouse. Now she watched Rex working silently, breathing slow and steady.

"Summer's over soon," she said.

Rex kept working.

"I may never know who my dad is."

Rex continued what he was doing.

"Maybe I don't care," she said.

Rex nodded absently. She watched the way his hands moved while he sanded the piece of wood. Rex had careful hands. True hands. He never undertook anything halfway. He never did something shoddily.

"I just, I admire him, you know?"

Rex looked up from what he was doing. "How?"

Murphy shrugged. "Because he didn't let me hold him back. He stayed true to himself." Rex shook his head and laughed under his breath. It was the kind of laugh that said he knew she'd never change. "I just . . . maybe I wish I were a little connected. Maybe I wish I had a permanent place on a wall somewhere."

Rex only stared at her.

"I know that makes no sense."

"It does."

Murphy felt an overwhelming urge to burrow in Rex's arms, to have the tactile experience of the cloth of his shirt against her cheek, and to have his smell wrap around her. She cleared her throat. The music on the radio changed to something slow.

"Rex, why were you at my house? With my mom?"

Rex glanced up at her. He seemed to think for a long moment. And then he stood up. "Wanna dance?" he asked.

Murphy stared for a moment, and then grinned, disbelievingly. "Here?"

"Yeah, sure, why not?"

Murphy looked around, feeling awkward, and then slid off her stool, shoving her hands in her pockets. Rex put down the slab of wood and stood, turned up the music, took her by the wrist, and led her out the great open door of the barn onto the grass.

He put one hand on her waist and the other in her right hand, holding it up.

"You were going to leave," Murphy said. "Without telling me."

"You left me first," Rex said.

"I'm sorry," she said. Murphy knew she could never be fully in New York if she was partly back here with him in her head. She couldn't have him—that was the problem. She only wanted to have him.

"I know that, Murphy." He pulled back and smiled at her. "It's okay. It's just a dance."

Something about it hurt Murphy. And something about it made her feel safer.

She allowed herself to rest her chin on his shoulder.

They danced like the grass did, rustling in the breeze.

As a child, Leeda Cawley-Smith had had a natural attachment to animals, and they had had a natural attachment to her—cats and dogs were constantly following her home and even squirrels let her get close enough to feed them nuts. Her grandmom, who loved petite, pretty ponies but who was certain that all other animals must be rabid, told her that if she didn't stop luring the animals with treats and cuddles, she'd get bitten and die. This claim made such an impression on Leeda that it created a distance between her and animals that continued to grow long after she had forgotten where it had come from. By the time she was ten years old, Leeda had forgotten, in fact, that she'd ever cared for them at all.

Twenty-seven

Wednesday night, Leeda woke to the sound of tiny pebbles hitting her window. She must have been dreaming about her grandmom, because her first sleep-soaked thought was that it was the mysterious M. of the letters trying to wake Eugenie. Sitting up, Leeda looked around the room and tried to orient herself, trying to remember where she was. She wasn't in the dorms and she wasn't at Primrose Cottage, and finally it sank in that she was in her bedroom at her parents' house.

She slid out from under the covers and stuck her face up against the screen, expecting to see Murphy or Birdie down below. But it was Grey who stood in a moonlit circle of grass.

Leeda backed up and pulled on her sweatshirt, worried. She thought about the animals and wondered who could be hurt and how she could handle it. Her heart was still sore from losing Barky. She tiptoed out of her room, blood throbbing in her eardrums.

She slinked past the room where Eric was sleeping, making sure she didn't wake him. She continued down the stairs, gliding like silk, and opened the front door slowly, slipping through the crack and out into the night air. She tentatively pulled it closed behind her.

Grey was standing near a tree across the grass. She hurried over.

"Is everything okay?" she whispered.

"Yeah, yeah, everything's fine."

"Are the ponies okay?"

"Ponies are great."

Leeda straightened up, relieved. "The dogs and everybody?"

"Yeah, the animals are fine."

Leeda waited for him to go on, but he didn't. She felt recognition then expectation dawning on her. He had something more to say to her. It was the way he was looking at her, like he was about to make a confession. She leaned against the tree to steady herself. She looked up at the sky.

Don't say it, she thought. *Don't make this uncomfortable.*

"I kissed Birdie today."

At first Leeda didn't know what he'd said. It didn't fit into anything she was expecting, so it sounded like gibberish.

"What?" she asked.

"We kissed."

Leeda's expression didn't change. But she felt suddenly, inexplicably like her skin was on fire. She felt unbearably, searingly hot.

"You kissed Birdie?"

Grey winced. "Leeda . . ." He looked lost. His hesitation gave Leeda all the time she needed to gather herself together.

"I don't understand," she said, her voice breezy while her heart raced. "I didn't know you liked Birdie." Leeda felt acutely abandoned. Like she was being left somewhere away and alone, and she hadn't seen it coming.

Grey looked like he'd lost his bearings. "C'mon, Leeda. Be real with me."

"What do you mean? You're so—"

Grey reached out and swept her hand into his. He looked at it like it was some kind of creature all its own. When he kissed her knuckles, it was like he was kissing a tiny animal.

Leeda felt her face flame hotter, and she slipped her hand out from where he held it. Not quickly, but as if it had never happened. Like she hadn't noticed. She didn't know why she couldn't act like she'd noticed. It was like she was in a cage inside herself.

"Well, I don't know why you woke me up to tell me, but I'm happy for you guys."

Grey kept staring at her hand. Disappointed. But not in himself. It was disappointment in her. In her cowardice. She could see it clear as day. If she was going to reject him, why couldn't she just be open about rejecting him? Why did she have to hide?

He swallowed. He took a step back. His face settled into a distant expression.

"I wanted you to hear it from me and not from Birdie."

Leeda stood tighter against her tree. They stared at each other.

"You said you don't know what you are. But you do," Grey said. "You just don't want to know you know. And it sucks because"—his voice cracked here, as if he was going to cry—"you're lucky. You've got so much more than most people."

He looked down and swiped at his nose, and Leeda stared at him, confused.

He squinted back at her like he was sizing her up.

"Good night."

She watched him cross the lawn, and then she crept back inside. She stood outside Eric's door, listening for his breathing. And then she continued down to her room. She crawled back into bed, facing the window with the moonlight still shining in. Her chest throbbed like it never had in her life.

Leeda had never been much into crying. But tears slid down her cheeks. She knew she had no reason for them, and she didn't understand them.

Leeda had had breakups. She had said good-byes to her friends. She had run over her friend's dog. She had been racked with guilt, longing, and hurt before. But she had never felt this specific kind of searing in her heart.

It was like becoming real.

Early the next morning, Leeda drove Eric to the airport. She hugged and kissed him good-bye, clinging tighter to him than ever.

Once he was gone, she reluctantly steered a course for Primrose Cottage. She dreaded seeing Grey. But pulling into the tiny driveway she saw, with relief, that his car wasn't there.

Inside, the animals greeted her. A parrot that had arrived that week, cage and all, squawked at her. The dogs—four of them now—launched into happy yips. One of the cats that had shown up on the porch rubbed itself against her legs.

"Oh God, I'm Dr. Dolittle," Leeda said out loud. She squeezed the door shut behind her and walked into the kitchen. There was an envelope by the coffeemaker with her name on it. Her stomach flopped. She turned it over, opened the flap, and slowly pulled out the letter.

Leeda,

I've gone to Alaska. I don't think I have to explain.

I understand why you want to be where you're going. Don't forget that being unsure isn't the same thing as being weak or aimless. Don't let anyone push you into thinking that the sure thing is also the true thing.

Please pass my apologies on to Birdie for leaving without talking to her, although I don't think she'll really care. I don't know what she's looking for, but I think I just happened to be standing in the way when she was looking for it.

You and the animals take care of each other.

Yours,
Grey

Leeda held the letter, dumbfounded. She walked back into the living room. She looked at the chaos of lives around her, dependent on her.

She sank onto the couch. Tufty, a recently arrived border terrier, jumped up on her lap, licking her face. Leeda pulled him close, suddenly, and held him, sinking her face into his ears, feeling the warmth of his body against hers, feeling guilty that he wasn't Barky but also feeling happy that he was there.

She couldn't imagine holding another person that way. It was love at its simplest.

Twenty-eight

Long ago, Birdie had gotten into the habit of having to walk to think, like moving her feet could supply power to her brain. So now, when she needed to sort things out in her head, she launched into a long hike around the perimeter of the farm.

Birdie had never been all that conventional, but she'd always been steady. She had never been one of those people who did things they couldn't explain. Those people had always seemed glamorous to Birdie—mysteriously complicated. But now she was one of those people, and it only felt foggy and ridiculous. She had done so many things, one on top of the other, that she didn't understand or have any reason for. Leaving Enrico. Living in a tree house. Kissing Grey. It was like she had separated from herself, and the part of her taking charge was a little crazy.

Up at the northwest corner of the property, there was a hollow oak where Birdie used to play as a little girl. She walked in that direction. When she saw legs poking out of the hole, she started. For a moment, she thought the dainty feet belonged to the ghost of her little self. And then she saw the tiny, almost imperceptible scars that marked the time Leeda had been swarmed by fire ants.

"I thought this was my tree," Birdie said, kneeling down and peering inside. Leeda was on her back, staring up into the hollowness above. Two of the newer dogs from the cottage, Tufty and Thelma Lou, lurched out to kiss her face.

"I heard your crutches coming," Leeda said. She shimmied out of the tree and sat up, bark and dirt stuck to her back.

"Why aren't you with the ponies?"

Leeda brushed the debris off her lap, looking around like someone who'd been sleeping. "I just wanted to be here." She picked up a piece of bark and oddly, Birdie noticed, stuck it in her shorts pocket.

She moved around to prop herself against the tree, and Birdie plunked down next to her, the bark digging into their backs and the roots pushing up under their butts.

"Bird? Grey left for Alaska."

Birdie squinted, an odd mixture of disappointment and relief running through her at the same time. "Really?"

Leeda nodded, staring toward the house. They could just see the back of the roof from here. It was like being in a different country than the peach rows—all grass and rolling hills, with only a scattering of tall, spindly trees, many of them draped in kudzu.

"I wonder if I have halitosis or something," Birdie mused. "Maybe I scared him away." She had read in a fashion magazine that if you licked your wrist and let it dry and then smelled it, you could tell if you had bad breath. She licked her wrist then looked over at Leeda, and the strange look on Leeda's face made her forget about it.

"Are you upset he's gone?"

Leeda quickly shook her head, her lips tightening. Birdie gazed at her for a moment. And something hit her.

"Lee." She tapped her hand against her forehead. "Oh my God." She rose up on her knees, slapping them animatedly with her hands. She sank back down, staring at Leeda's face, which was impassive and far away. "You like him."

"No."

"I mean . . ." Birdie rapidly put little pieces together. "I guess I could tell he liked you. I just never thought about it much because you . . . didn't seem . . . and Eric and all. Ugh. I mean, Lee, he's not interested in me. I'm not interested in him. I don't even know why I kissed him. It was like . . ." Birdie waggled her hands in the air like a TV evangelist. "It was like a compulsion."

"It's not that," Leeda said, giving Birdie a smile that was both hurt and forgiving.

Birdie sank back, confused.

"Then why do you look like that?" Leeda's face was usually smooth and calm even when, Birdie knew, she was suffering. But right now, she had a raw, confused expression, as if something had been peeled away from her.

"I don't know what's wrong. I feel . . . like I have something important. Like I can see something about myself better than I ever have or something. But when I try to focus on it, it disappears. It's like when there's a song on the tip of your tongue but trying to remember it only makes it get lost in your head."

Birdie stared at her, not sure she understood. "What is it?" she asked.

Leeda rolled her hands together, kneading them against each

other. "I don't know. I just . . . I'm not ready to go back to the city. And that's crazy."

Leeda looked down at her tiny red slip-on shoes and pulled at the elastics.

"Do you think it's normal, Birdie, to love a piece of the ground? I just love this piece of ground we're sitting on."

Though Leeda's question came out of the blue, Birdie understood it deeply. "Poopie says everything has a soul. Even a brick. Even a piece of grass or a place. I think when they take down my house, it'll be like when Honey Babe died. It will be like losing someone. Maybe I'm crazy, but that's how it feels."

Birdie gestured helplessly with her left hand then let it loll on her lap. Leeda stared at where she was still wearing her ring.

Birdie followed her gaze. "It's pretty nice to think of something being forever." She looked toward the roofline of the house, and then took in the rest of the area with her gaze. "I kind of thought this was. You know, home and everything. But I guess it's not."

She glanced back down at her ring. And for the first time, it felt completely real that in three weeks' time, they wouldn't be here anymore.

"Hey, Lee?"

"Yeah."

"Will you take me somewhere?"

Twenty-nine

$\mathcal{B}$irdie stared at the Departures board at Atlanta's Hartsfield Airport, clutching her luggage tote, which contained her teddy-bear suitcase and a giant plush peach she'd just bought at the gift shop. She'd had two Frappuccinos, savoring every sugary mouthful, and now she wondered how she was going to manage to spend the next several hours sitting still on a plane. She suspected that she might have to hop up and do a jig in the aisle, sprained ankle and all.

Birdie loved planes. She loved airports. She loved people with luggage. She loved knowing she was going somewhere.

It had been easy to slip away from everyone. She'd told her dad and Poopie she was staying at her mom's. She'd told her mom she was going away camping with Murphy. She had dipped into her school savings for the second time in her life. Granted, last-minute flights to and from Mexico didn't exactly make a small dent. But Birdie figured this was life-and-death. So it was worth it.

On the flight she watched two movies, but her mind kept drifting to Enrico. His easy laugh. His concentration when he was reading a book. The way it felt when she laid back against him while they were watching TV and he wrapped his arms around her.

Birdie fiddled nervously with her ring, her thumb moving over the tiny diamonds, one-two-three, one-two-three. She stared out the window, looking down at the clouds, wondering what part of the earth they were over, what tiny island, what ocean, and were there sharks directly beneath her somewhere? Or a whale?

Finally her sugar level crashed, and her brain stopped running a mile a minute. She held her giant peach—a present for Enrico—to her like a pillow and tried to sleep to make the hours pass.

By the time Birdie landed in Mexico City, seven hours after she'd left, she felt like she'd lived a lifetime on the plane. She hobbled along to the baggage claim to get her suitcase and emerged into the hectic stand of taxis and cars and buses in the queue outside, noticing the change in the air immediately. It was hotter and thicker in Mexico City.

She awkwardly crammed herself and her stuff into the backseat of a cab, flopping onto the giant peach like a sloth and directing the driver to Enrico's family's village. When they'd last talked, that was where he was spending the summer.

She watched the now-familiar highway roadside sweep past the cab, rushing her to her future. Again the ride went on endlessly. It was a full hour and a half's drive to Enrico's house. Her heart picked up its pace when they finally pulled off the main road onto a bumpy side street and Enrico's neighborhood came into view.

Birdie tottered out of the cab, paid the driver, and hoisted her peach into her arms. All the way across the grass, she kept dropping it and having to pick it up, which with her crutches took about a minute each time.

She found the family around back. Apparently all of Enrico's relatives, including second cousins, were over for a barbecue. Several of them looked up at her curiously.

Enrico was standing over the grill with his back to her. But his mom, seeing Birdie, tapped him on the arm. He turned, and when he saw her, he looked like he was happy to see her and at the same time not quite sure she was real.

Birdie nodded and smiled unsurely at everyone as Enrico crossed the grass toward her. He looked her up and down, taking in her crutches, and then leaned forward stiffly to give her a tiny, awkward hug. He glanced over his shoulder at the grill, where his mom had now taken over, and then at his relatives, self-conscious. They were still watching them, but it was only between talking and chewing mouthfuls of food.

"What are you doing here?" Enrico asked, his gaze turning back to Birdie.

Birdie smiled widely. "Enrico," she whispered excitedly, looking him square in the eye and ignoring the onlookers. "I want to get married."

Enrico jerked slightly. He looked back at his relatives again as if he hoped they hadn't heard, and then back at Birdie, whose heart was beating wildly. She forced herself to go on.

"I'm so sorry," she said. "I got scared. But I'm ready now. I know this is how it's supposed to be."

Enrico's Adam's apple bobbed as he leaned closer. He took

her hand and stared at it. "Birdie . . . I think we should go inside and talk."

"I'm saying yes." She beamed at him, waiting for it to sink in and for the relieved smile to spread over his face. He tugged her hand gently, trying to pull her toward the house, but Birdie only wobbled and stayed put. She felt like it mattered that she didn't move. She wanted to stand her ground.

Enrico finally realized she wasn't budging, and his shoulders dropped, resigned. He smiled at her and spoke very quietly.

"Birdie." He wrapped his fingers around hers tightly. "You don't want to marry me."

"I do." Birdie nodded. "I do!" She had never been so sure of anything. It was like everything that had happened suddenly meant something. She was supposed to be here. That made all the other things okay.

But Enrico's expression wasn't happy. It wasn't even getting close.

"You don't want to marry me," he pressed, sounding sure of himself, like this was something that he couldn't be dissuaded from. "You only want something to be sure."

Birdie swallowed. She felt like she was taking a hit. She shook her head. "That's not true."

"It's okay, Birdie. I . . ." He shook his head slightly. He looked up at her from under his eyebrows, like he was very sorry. "I don't want to get married either."

Finally, too late, it occurred to Birdie that this whole grand plan could fail. She could walk away empty-handed. And now the possibility loomed up, huge and real. And not just real—suddenly likely.

She swallowed and, with a sick feeling, glanced over at Mrs. Fiol tending the barbecue. Then she looked back at Enrico.

"But . . . you asked me?" she said, numb.

"I thought it was what you wanted. And what I wanted too. You seem to need . . . to know things. I understand this about you."

Birdie's throat ached. "You think I'm a coward."

Enrico shook his head furiously.

"That's what you're saying." Birdie's feet felt floaty. She felt like she could drift into the air like a balloon.

"I thought a lot this summer," Enrico said. "I never gave up hoping that you would come back. But I still thought that we are so young. We have all this space to be free."

He was so calm. How could he be so calm?

"Free," Birdie echoed. It seemed like a small consolation next to being loved and safe. It seemed like nothing to her.

Birdie focused, suddenly, on the relatives across the lawn. Was she imagining it, or did they look like they felt sorry for her? The drifting feeling intensified, and she suddenly felt as if she were floating above her own body. Who was that girl with the crutches looking like a total idiot? And why was she holding a giant peach?

Birdie needed to get away immediately. And she needed to leave with whatever dignity she had left.

"That's fine," she said, nodding. "I hope freedom keeps you from . . . being cold," she spat. She'd been reaching for a "keeps you warm at night" line she'd heard on *Days of Our Lives,* but it hadn't come out right. "You know, in the winter!" She could feel her cheeks flaming and turning red. She lifted her chin, as if she were above it all. "Well, gotta go," she said airily.

She turned to leave and started to hobble away. She could hear the sounds of the barbecue continuing without her. She tried to ignore the sudden thought that a minute ago, Enrico's family had seemed like they would be her family too, and now they were strangers who probably thought she was a huge loser.

Out on the front lawn, she suddenly stopped short and goggled at the empty road. It took a minute for her to realize what was missing and why. And then, when she realized it, she wanted to kick herself. How could she have forgotten?

She threw her peach on the grass, waggled her arms a few times in silent rage, and then leaned on her crutches and hobbled around to the back of the house again. She didn't look left or right to see where Enrico had gone, she merely spurred herself toward Enrico's mom where she stood by the grill.

Mrs. Fiol turned with a spatula in her hand, surprised.

Without looking her in the eye, Birdie forced the words out. "Um, can I have a ride to the airport?"

Thirty

From where Murphy, Leeda, and Birdie sat in the tree house, the bonfire looked like a small burning sun, casting orange light and shadows onto the white siding of the dorms. To Murphy, it appeared as though the workers were having some kind of pagan ritual.

All around the orchard that week, people had been saying their good-byes. Picking had slowed to a crawl. The workers pulled peaches from the trees as if it were an afterthought, distractedly daydreaming, talking to each other in low voices that still carried through the rows as tiny murmurs.

Murphy hadn't exactly realized she had favorite trees, but she did, and she imagined the others did too because she sometimes saw them running their hands along certain trunks or holding branches in their fingers gently, like hands.

The girls had hung back from the bonfire, as if going would make tomorrow—when the bus came to gather everyone up for Mexico—come faster. From here the crickets were extra loud, talking from all their little homes in the tree's branches. Leeda was stretched out next to Birdie's mattress with her arm dangling off the side of the platform, as if she were in a boat and letting her fingers loll in the water.

A few tiny lights began to blink below.

"Hey, Bird," Leeda murmured. "Aren't those the synchronous fireflies?"

Birdie nodded.

"Don't you think they're magic or something?" Murphy asked.

"I don't know," Birdie said. She fondled the foamy top of one of her crutches, which she had stopped using when she'd gotten back from Mexico.

"I'm hungry," Murphy finally said. "C'mon."

She jumped up then turned to pull Birdie up by both hands. Leeda disappeared down the ladder ahead of them.

The group around the fire welcomed them with smiles. Poopie forced a giant plate of food into Murphy's hands: rice wrapped in corn husks, peach chutney, mashed black beans in a spicy brown sauce. She sat on a log next to one of the guys and dug in.

It was obviously a party that would last long into the night. Stories were exchanged, some in English so Leeda and Murphy could understand better, although by now their Spanish was passable. Everyone had a story about the Darlingtons or the orchard, some that even made Walter laugh from where he sat, tucked between Poopie and Luis.

About an hour after they'd sat down, Murphy went to the house to use the bathroom, because it was easier than making her way through the crowd to the door of the dorm. When she came out, she got to the edge of the driveway before she stopped.

She took in the scene before her, everybody laughing and occasionally wiping away their tears.

She suddenly decided she didn't want to sleep near the others tonight. She wanted to remember everyone like this, when she could still picture them sitting at the fire enjoying each other. She pulled her bike off its kickstand.

Orchard Road smelled like honeysuckle and was full of frogs warming themselves on the concrete that still held the sun's heat. Murphy swerved to miss them as she rode home and pulled into her driveway.

She immediately hit the brakes with her heels, staring at Rex's truck, which was parked in front of her trailer.

There were people on her front stoop, and she took them all in at once: her mom, Rex, and Judge Abbott, in the process of parting. Murphy could only blink at the scene, trying to make sense of it. They were talking in tense tones.

"... won't help anything. She doesn't need ..."

Murphy couldn't make out more. She climbed off her bike and stepped forward, her insides swirling.

The three on the stoop turned in surprise. Her mom's look of anger turned to one of guilt. Rex's brow furrowed, and he met her eyes directly.

"Hi, Murphy," Judge Abbott said first. There was a strange tone in his voice. "We were just talking about you."

Murphy didn't say anything. She knew it was coming whether she asked or not now. Judge Abbott came down the stairs. Murphy had the strangest feeling. She didn't want to know anymore. She knew that whatever he was going to say was going to hurt.

"Your mother doesn't think it's good for you and that you don't need to hear this. But it's really important to me—"

Rex was suddenly down the stairs. "Leave it alone, please," he said, standing in front of Murphy. Judge Abbott looked at him, confused, and then he went on.

"I ordered a paternity test about three months ago. I knew you'd be coming home from school—"

Rex's fist shot out of nowhere. He got in one good punch before Jodee yelped and ran forward to grab his arm. Murphy couldn't believe her eyes. It was like a cartoon. Rex Taggart fighting Judge Abbott in the parking lot of Anthill Acres. Jodee's touch seemed to bring Rex back to his senses, and the two men pulled away from each other, panting.

"Murphy," Judge Abbott said between labored breaths, "I'm your dad."

Murphy didn't know why, but the only thought that went through her head was of Darth Vader in *Star Wars*. She tried to imagine Judge Abbott saying, "I am your father," all breathily. She thought he must be joking.

But this was no joke. She could tell, because Judge Abbott was no joker. And because everyone was looking at her as if they were waiting on her next move.

Murphy took a deep, frantic breath. She felt what she imagined a person would feel if they'd just walked in on someone cheating on them. Utterly shocked. Utterly betrayed.

Her eyes wandered to Rex.

"You knew?" she asked.

Rex, still breathing heavily, looked too distraught to speak.

Murphy didn't look at Judge Abbott. She didn't care to look at him. She looked at her mother and at Rex, back and forth between them, seeing something in both of them she'd never imagined.

And then she got on her bike and took off.

Thirty-one

Leeda hung up the phone in the kitchen and stared at it, relieved. In a few short days of nonstop work, she had finally managed to do what she hadn't been able to do all summer. She had found a place for the ponies.

It was going to take a while to sink in. It was a place in Tennessee. She'd have to make three trips with the trailer. But it was a done deal. It felt like the day she'd finished her last exams at school in the spring. Like she couldn't believe all that stuff she'd pored over was suddenly off her hands.

The other animals were a different story. Leeda felt buried. She hadn't found a place for them and didn't know how she would. She had talked to the people at the ASPCA, but they couldn't vouch for the future of the animals or whether they would be put to sleep or not. So she was holding on to them, hoping for some lightbulb to go off in her head.

The animals were all wide awake and talking to each other. Leeda had almost gotten used to the constant barking and meowing and antics of the most rambunctious ones. Minxy the cat—like most of the animals, named by Birdie—liked to do little rolls on the carpet, showing her belly to get Leeda's attention whenever she passed her pen. Tufty howled as if his life was ending, until Leeda stopped and pet him for a few minutes, resuming the moment she walked away.

Leeda ducked upstairs amid the clatter and into her grand-mom's room. She was half packed, busy clearing out all the things that had migrated over the summer from the orchard and from her parents' house to the cottage. She hovered in front of her grandmom's open closet, trying to pick out what was hers among the stuffed clothes bulging from the hangers. Her eyes wandered up to the box of letters on the shelf. She still hadn't decided what to do with it.

A commotion downstairs distracted her. She hurried down to the living room. One of the cats had snuck out of the cat room and was hissing, his back arched, at the dogs, who were going crazy in their pens trying to get at her.

Leeda groaned and put her back in the cat enclosure that she'd made out of Eugenie's dining room. "Bad cat," she said, looking at Minxy sternly. "How are you getting out?" Then she got to work.

First there were the indoor animals. Leeda took all five dogs out on their leashes, letting herself be dragged along as they sniffed at this rock, trotted to that tree, and wrestled with one another exuberantly. She smiled, watching them. They were like clowns. Constantly ridiculous. Once she managed to drag them back inside and foist each dog into its pen, she filled all the food and water bowls. She cleaned the parrot cage and managed not to feel like gagging. She rubbed the parrot on the back of his head, which she'd discovered was his favorite spot. She thought about

Birdie catching impetigo from her chicken. She could see now how one might not be totally disgusted to kiss a bird. The parrot looked at her with such human curiosity. Birdie had named him Chiquito and had nuzzled her nose to his. Now Leeda tried it, half afraid she'd lose her nose. But Chiquito nestled into her and made a low sound of contentment in the back of his throat.

Outside, the weather had shifted. The edge was off the heat. Leeda could feel it on her way to the corral.

The ponies looked mopey today, their ears down with no signs of friskiness. It was as though ennui had caught them all like a cold. They needed feeding, watering, brushing, cleaning. Leeda lugged bucket after bucket from the spigot to the water troughs, the muscles behind her shoulder blades pulling and stretching. She shoveled the manure out of each stable, occasionally swiping at her brow. Still, the ponies only stared pensively at her from their knot by the fence.

Sneezy especially seemed melancholy and needy. She broke away from the others and shadowed Leeda's every move—through the dusty stables and out to where the farthest trough sat under the shade of the trees. Leeda absently stroked her muzzle from time to time during her work. She fell into the rhythm of the shoveling, the carrying, and the pouring. It was almost meditative, like picking peaches. She felt her hands on the metal of the buckets and the wood of the stable doors. She felt Sneezy's breath as she petted her and breathed in her smell. Time boiled down to her immediate surroundings, and she forgot about Grey, Eric, New York, the future, and the upcoming day when she'd take the ponies to Tennessee.

She stopped only at midday, when the sun was at its highest, for some shade and a sandwich. Then she tackled moving one of the feed troughs out from where it had been catching rain. She tried to drag it. No luck. She tried to push it from the back. Still nothing. She fell back in the muck, exhausted. Sneezy eyed her, looking half amused.

She stood up again, tried again. Frustration pulsed through her body. Finally she fell forward with a grunt. And then she lost control. She started kicking the trough and jumping up and down. When she ran out of breath, she sank down cross-legged on the hay. Sneezy walked over and stood next to her, sniffing her cheek.

"I didn't tell him to leave," she said ruefully, with a sense of how comically sad the whole thing was. She was on her own, and inept, and her entire body was covered in mud. How had she gone from a year at Columbia University to this?

Sneezy snuffled. Leeda smiled and pressed her nose against the pony's. And then, from the direction of the house, she heard a bloodcurdling scream.

She was at the porch in an instant, taking the stairs two at once and rushing through the open front door, then skidding to a stop before she slammed into her visitor.

Lucretia was planted in the middle of the living room, gaping and grasping for words. All she could do, it seemed, was point. Point at the Oriental rug covered in feathers and fur and mud and bird poo. Point at the metal crates full of barking, meowing, whining animals. Point at Minxy, who had managed to get out again, lounging across the back of the piano like a songstress from the forties.

Feathers flew through the air. There was a mysterious trail of small muddy prints that could have belonged to any of the animals.

"Mom, I can explain."

"Ruined!" Lucretia said. "You've ruined your grandmother's house."

She turned to Leeda, and Leeda was shocked to see tears in her eyes. "My mother's house! Oh, Leeda, how could you? How could you show so little respect?"

Leeda swallowed. Never, in the whole time she'd been taking in the animals, had she even considered she was doing something that would hurt her mother. But now, looking around, she could see why she was so upset.

Thelma Lou let out a yip.

"Mom, I'm so sorry. I didn't think."

Lucretia shook her head in awe, devastated.

"What is this? Why?" she asked.

"I was just trying to help," Leeda said.

"Help who?"

"The animals."

Lucretia nodded, clearly collecting herself and becoming reasonable. "Leeda, this is out of control."

"I know."

"They need to go—immediately."

"I know."

"Within the week."

"It's taken care of, Mom."

"And then you need to fix this."

Leeda nodded. But Lucretia was raising a finger, pointing to a place on the shelf across the room.

"Where's your grandmother's egg?" she asked.

Leeda looked at her. She bit her bottom lip, and tiny tears welled up in her eyes. "It's broken, Mom. I'm sorry. I broke it."

Lucretia stared at her for another minute, and then walked to the door, shaking her head.

"I don't want to see this place again until it's perfect." She looked incredibly disappointed.

"Okay."

Leeda watched her mom leave, then closed the door behind her. She sank against the wood.

After a few minutes, her eyes drifted to the stairs. She suddenly stood up and walked to her grandmom's room.

She looked up again at the letters on the shelf. She thought about the messy, chaotic feelings they held. She had the wild urge to protect her grandmother, especially the parts of her that hadn't been perfect or pristine. She pulled the box down and poured its contents into the mesh pocket on the inside of her suitcase.

She would be the keeper of Eugenie's secrets.

Thirty-two

*B*irdie ran around all morning, getting the workers ready to go. There was so much to do that Birdie hardly had to think about the actual leaving. Before she knew it, the bus was pulling in.

She felt the moment upon her suddenly. And then she was wrapped up in hugs and *te amo*s and *Dios te acompaña*s. God be with yous. Within five minutes, they all had squashed themselves into the bus and the door was closing behind them. Birdie looked over. Poopie was crying, with Birdie's dad's arm wrapped around her, waving.

The bus pulled out, its passengers looking like a group of kids leaving an amusement park. There were loud shouts, songs, and a radio playing. They pulled to the end of the driveway, slowed for a second, turned right, and they were gone.

Poopie turned, sucking in great gulps of air between her tears, and walked into the house. Birdie felt her dad's hand on her shoulder.

They didn't say anything to each other for a few seconds; they just watched where the bus had been. Birdie's dad gave her shoulder a squeeze. And then he turned and followed Poopie inside.

Birdie stood aimlessly for a moment, and then she wandered into the peach trees, walking until she came out on the other side at the lake.

She clambered up onto the rock at the edge of what used to be the water. The hot summer had almost dried it up. Murphy had jumped off this rock when they'd first gone swimming together. Leeda's mother had lost a Barbie in the deep crevice that nearly split the rock in half. Birdie sat, looking at the muddy grass, twirling her ring around her finger.

She had been to a church once where someone had laid their crutches at the foot of a statue of the Virgin Mary. The story went that the person had been healed and had walked away, free of the thing they'd been bound to for so long. She pulled her ring off, staring at it thoughtfully. And then she held it over the crevice and dropped it in.

She wanted to leave a piece of herself here. Maybe that would be enough.

At the house, she stood at the bottom of her tree, staring up at it. She climbed up the ladder and unmade her bed. She grabbed an armful of books and started to carry them down.

Slowly she took the house apart, piece by piece.

Thirty-three

"Do you think they want this?" Murphy asked, holding up a cookbook with a French guy wearing a beret and holding an armful of pastries. "I mean, I think it's from 1960."

Leeda looked up from where she was crouching in front of the pantry, her hair pulled back in a thin white scarf that was tied at the nape of her neck, her face freckled from the sunshine but pale white underneath, like she hadn't slept. She shrugged.

Murphy gazed at the book then loaded it into the open box in front of her, next to the rest of the contents of the shelf. Little by little, they were packing up the Darlingtons' house.

"What did they do when they saw how many you had?" Murphy asked.

"The lady at the front desk was speechless."

Leeda had taken her animals to the pound the day before. She looked like someone had punched her in the stomach. Murphy had never seen her looking quite so empty. She moved like a piece of string.

They heard the clatter of Birdie upstairs, packing her room.

"I'm sorry, Lee."

Leeda laid her hands on her knees, chasing her breath. She couldn't seem to catch it, though.

Murphy loaded the last cookbook into the crate and picked it up. She carried it to the door, dropping it on the porch and dusting off her hands.

Her eyes drifted to the driveway.

"Crap."

Judge Abbott's car was parked next to Leeda's. He walked toward the dorms and disappeared around the corner. Murphy debated running back into the house, but she decided on making a break for the endless peach rows instead, running across the yard into the trees far enough to be hidden from sight.

From where she crouched, she had an obstructed view of the yard. She saw the judge walk across the grass to the house and poke his head through the open door, reluctant and polite. Leeda appeared a moment later and shook her head, her hands in the pockets of her shorts. He looked around then started walking, to her surprise, into the rows toward her. Murphy hit the deck, lying belly down on the grass. He disappeared into some trees to her left. Murphy laid her cheek on her hands and waited, watching an ant walking up and down a blade of grass. The smell of dirt tickled her nose. She could hear the judge's distant footsteps. And then suddenly a pair of shiny brown loafers was in front of her face, and she realized the distant footsteps must be Walter's. These shoes belonged to Judge Abbott.

Murphy looked up, shielding her face from the sun, and then stood.

"Hey, Judge."

"Murphy."

"What's going on?" She stuck her hands in her pockets and looked around, her face stone.

"I was wondering if you'd like to go to a movie with me tonight. Maybe have dinner. Talk a little bit."

"No thanks." Everything about Judge Abbott annoyed Murphy. The way he looked at her so intently. His loafers. He reminded her of her third-grade teacher.

The judge looked nervous, sheepish, and deeply sad. "I called you."

Murphy just tugged absently on a nearby branch.

Judge Abbott looked distinctly uncomfortable. "I . . . I've been wanting to give you these."

He put a little box into her hands.

Murphy took the box and stuck it in her back pocket, expressionless. If she had been hurt or angry with him, she would have thrown them back in his face. But she wasn't angry. She just felt kind of bad for him. "Okay. Thanks. Well, see ya."

"Murphy, I always wanted you. I wanted to be your dad. I talked to your mom about it when you were really small, after I'd figured it out. But I had gotten married by that point. And she said she didn't want you to be second to anyone. And she didn't want to do the test then to make sure. I respected her wishes."

"Please." Murphy held up her hand in a stop motion. "I don't want to know. I don't care. It's water under the bridge."

"I promise you, Murphy, I never would have made you second. When my wife died . . . it felt like enough was enough. But Jodee didn't feel . . ."

Murphy started walking. She walked straight down the row, across the grass, and into the house, closing the door behind her.

"Ballerinas."

"What?" Jodee McGowen stood in the kitchen looking lost. She stared at the ballerina earrings Murphy had laid on the counter.

"Ballerina earrings. That's what the judge just gave me."

"Murphy, I know you're mad. But Miller has always looked out for you. All those times you got in trouble? You know that. And he's always wanted to be part of your life, but I always resisted. And then he was married and, you know . . ."

"I'm not mad about any of that."

"Then what is it?"

Murphy looked down at her fists, clenched on the counter. "Why did it have to be someone like that, Mom? Why does it have to be him?"

"What are you talking about? Why not him?"

"He's so . . . awful! He wears loafers. He's got a house in a sub-division. He's a sellout. Just an ordinary, boring sellout."

Her mother looked bewildered. "Sellout?" She leaned a hand on the counter and narrowed her eyes, her words coming out twangy with emotion. "You'd rather he be someone who skipped out on you. That's better than somebody reliable? Somebody . . . good? Someone who tried to be there for you. That's what you're saying?"

Murphy didn't know. She felt all twisted up inside.

"Murphy, don't you expect more for yourself than just . . . being unencumbered?"

Murphy wanted to respond bitingly, but everything she thought of sounded too dramatic. She was free. She didn't owe anyone. "I can do anything I want," she said.

"What about the things that matter more?" Jodee asked.

Murphy bit her bottom lip, unconvinced, angry.

"I don't want these," she said, handing her mom the earrings. "And I don't want him. Can you please just give these back and tell him that?"

Her mom looked at her, resigned. Murphy knew the look well.

It was the look of someone expecting more from her.

Thirty-four

It was surprising how many people showed up on the day the Darlington farmhouse was to be demolished. Some people came whom Birdie had never seen. She wasn't sure why they would have come at all. An auction for the property was set for Saturday, and maybe some of them had come to see it all firsthand. But ultimately, it was hard to say why they were all there.

It was only a house. It was only a day.

The bulldozer sat at attention, ready to go. Walter was holding Poopie's hand. Leeda and Murphy and Birdie's mom stood behind Birdie, but nobody touched her. Nobody tried to hold her hand. She must have been giving off the impression of being an island.

From where they all stood in the grass behind a yellow piece of tape, Birdie watched the contractor come out of the house for the last time and walk down the saggy front stairs. Casually, he walked over and talked to a man standing by the bulldozer. The man looked up at the driver, said something, and nodded to him.

Birdie had resolved to stand there and take it like an adult. She didn't decide to do what she did. She just did it. When she saw the operator reach for the key of the bulldozer, she ducked under the tape and ran for the house.

At first she thought she might lie down on the front porch and be a human shield. But instead, moving on some deep impulse, she opened the door and ran inside, slamming it behind her. She ran up the stairs to her bedroom. She swooped down into the corner by the window, wrapped her arms around her knees, and began to cry.

Birdie cried like she hadn't cried since she was five years old. She cried for the workers that were gone, and for Honey Babe the dead dog, and for the caves under the house, and for Enrico. She cried for the simple fact that people lost things that mattered.

She knew they were outside thinking she was ridiculous, but she didn't care. She planted her hands on the wooden floor of her room and cried her heart out.

When she finally looked up from her knees, Poopie was kneeling beside her. Behind her were her mom, Leeda, and Murphy. They didn't look like they thought she was ridiculous.

"Avelita," Poopie whispered. "Avelita, there. It's okay."

Birdie stared at Poopie for a second, then wrapped her arms around her neck and cried some more. Poopie didn't laugh at her or tell her to buck up. She rubbed her hair like she completely understood. Like she understood everything.

"Are they gonna knock the house down and kill us all?" She sniffled through her hair against Poopie's shoulder.

"We could go down with the ship," her mom said, reaching

down to stroke Birdie's hair. Birdie laughed through her tears and sat back, rubbing her eyes.

"I feel like a little kid," she said, sniffling and looking down at the floor.

"That's okay," Poopie said.

Leeda and Murphy crawled forward and sank back against the wall next to Birdie. Poopie and Cynthia did too, on the other side.

They sat staring at the opposite wall, thinking their own thoughts, which all revolved around the same basic things.

"I could go for a Nicorette," Murphy said, and Leeda snorted. Birdie laughed too.

A few minutes went by until they pulled one another up.

One by one, they filed out.

Birdie turned around to look at her room. She didn't know where she was going now, but she knew it felt like jumping off a cliff. For the first time ever, she couldn't see what was waiting for her.

She turned and followed.

All in all, thirty-two people watched the Darlington farmhouse get knocked to the ground. A few of them cried. Several of them shook their heads, thinking it was the end of some kind of era they hadn't even known was an era. Within fifteen minutes, they saw a hundred-year-old house reduced to a pile of rubble on the ground.

Afterward, everyone stood and stared at one another like creatures in shock. And then they began to trickle away to go about their lives. If you had asked them tomorrow what they'd done the day before, half of them would have had to think for a minute to remember that yes, they'd gone to see a demolition.

Only a few of them thought they saw shapes in the clouds on the drive home. And the shapes were faint—of things they couldn't quite name and hadn't seen yet.

Thirty-five

Leeda peered through the open doors of the trailer, making sure everyone was situated. Mitzie and The Baron were the backmost two ponies, and The Baron snuffed at her, stretching out his neck to sniff her shirt and give it a tiny nibble. Leeda placed her hand assertively on his muzzle and gave him a nudge so he wouldn't chew a hole in the fabric. She leaned down and nosed him, smelling his scent.

"They'll take good care of you," she said. Still, she couldn't look him in the eye. Closing the trailer doors, she turned and walked inside. The living room, but for a few pens that needed to be disassembled and taken outside, was pristine and quiet. It felt empty, like a room that had just been vacated, even though the animals had been gone for days. But it looked perfect.

She checked the answering machine one more time—nothing but a few saved messages from Eric, the last one saying he'd see her at the airport in four days. She went upstairs to grab her purse. She sat on the bed. The house felt as silent as if it were buried underground. Leeda had never heard such quiet in her life. She had never felt more alone.

She thought, since this was her last chance, that she might take something more of her grandmom's with her. One last magpie item for the road. She opened the top drawer of Eugenie's chest and looked through her jewelry, searching for something small and cheap, without any value to anyone but her. The jewelry box had two compartments, one on top of the other. Leeda pulled off the top layer and stopped, peering down at an envelope.

It was another letter. Leeda studied it curiously. She wondered why it was apart from all the others.

She slid it out of the yellowish envelope, opened it, and read.

Genie—

I can't wait for you anymore.

If I don't hear from you by tomorrow night, I'll know what you've decided to keep, and I won't blame you. But I'll be gone by the morning. It's too hard to be here anymore.

If I never see you again, I just want to hope one thing for you. I want to hope you won't be afraid. Of whatever or whomever you love. I hope courage for you.

,

Your Mandie Rae

Leeda stared at the letter, utterly blank. Mandie Rae? Her brain moved slowly over the very simple truth, as though the wheels in her head had started running slower. A woman. Her grandmother had loved a woman.

Leeda swallowed. She sat for several minutes, absorbing it. She stared at the full signature again. It was probably the reason

Eugenie had kept this letter hidden and separate. Her lover had had the courage to sign her full name.

Leeda let out a shuddering, angry sigh. *They had never had a chance,* she thought, her head spinning. Not with Eugenie being who she was. It would have been a slim chance for anyone. But for Eugenie—perfect and respectable—it would have been almost impossible.

Finally she put the letter into its envelope and folded it into her pocket, holding it tightly in her fist.

A heavy weight bore down on her as she walked to the trailer. Maybe part of her had hoped something else for the two of them, despite what history told her. But it was the difficulty of their love that dragged at her. It was senseless. In a different kind of world they could have let themselves be happy. But in the world her grandmom had lived in, brick walls had stood firmly between Eugenie and true happiness.

Leeda pulled on her raincoat, hoisted up her bags, and headed out the front door, locking it behind her with a knot in her throat.

She put her stuff in the passenger seat and climbed into the driver's side, looking behind her to make sure the trailer was okay before starting the ignition and slowly backing out. A few knickknacks sat on the dashboard where Leeda had placed them to make room in her purse for a water bottle. Her Miss Piggy. The half a crayon. Some bark.

She drove about twenty-five miles per hour, so it took forever to get down Main Street. Then she was crawling out Anjaco Road, past the grainery, and toward the fairgrounds. A sign loomed up on her in rainbow letters: AUCTION TODAY!

She had seen the sign a million times. There were auctions at the fairgrounds every Saturday. Today, she knew, they were auctioning the orchard. Because of the weather, the grounds would be muddy. It would be miserable. Just the way it should be.

The sign crawled past her, and then she was on empty road, just trees on either side.

Her mind turned back to it, though. Again and again, she came back to the sign. On her right, the town dump, where people left used tires and appliances and all their trash, was approaching.

Suddenly, forgetting the trailer behind her, Leeda made a sharp, sudden turn into the dump. She swiveled in her seat to make sure the trailer had stayed hitched.

She sat for a moment, staring at the windshield wipers breathlessly, the knot in her throat huge, tears springing to her eyes. And then she swiped at them, sniffed, gathered herself, and pulled a wide U-turn, back onto the road the way she'd come. She pressed harder on the gas. As she drove faster, an irrepressible smile grew on her face, and her heart raced in pure, unadulterated fear.

She had just realized there was somewhere else she was supposed to be.

A year before she died, Eugenie Cawley-Smith was sitting on her porch, reading a box of old letters and crying. When a neighbor stopped to ask her what was wrong, she hit him in the shin with her cane, and she walked inside to put her secrets where they belonged.

Thirty-six

Murphy looked at the address and then up at the house. In all the years she'd known her dad, she'd never known where he lived.

It was a cookie-cutter house. Two floors, green siding, and a small, square yard. It didn't have the slightest hint of personality. At least the trailer had a certain rusty romanticism to it. Murphy sighed, kicked her feet at the pavement a few times, considered leaving, and finally walked up to the door. The screen door was closed, but the door itself was open to the late August air, the sounds of kids playing down the street, or the occasional distant honk of a horn. Murphy peered into the darkness. Somewhere inside, a TV was on. She looked at the doorbell, and then at the black cast metal door handle. On impulse, she pushed the thumb button and opened the door.

She followed the sound to the living room, where her dad was sitting on a beige sofa. He started when he saw her.

"Hey." Before he could get up, she plopped down on the couch next to him. "What're you watching?"

He took a moment to gather himself, then answered, "*Matlock* reruns." He sat back, looking at her askance. Murphy just stared at the TV. Finally he turned to the TV too. From her spot on the couch, Murphy could see the empty dining room, a light on in the kitchen, and a pile of papers on the kitchen table that had to be his work. She hadn't ever pictured the judge as lonely. But she had imagined the quiet of his house.

The judge reached for a bag of chips that was sitting on the table beside him and offered them to Murphy. Murphy took a few, and he put the bag between them so she could have more. It was a nice, dependable thing to do.

Halfway through the show, when she was starting to feel sleepy, she laid her head on his shoulder. It felt slightly awkward and slightly pleasant.

"I'm sorry I called you a chump," she said.

"It's okay," he replied.

"Even though only a chump watches *Matlock*."

Her dad laughed. He had a kind of dorky, understated, controlled laugh that reminded Murphy of the fact that he was a judge and that he probably thought he had a reputation to uphold, even around those he loved.

It didn't feel wild or free.

But it felt like real life.

Maybe sometimes, real was enough.

irdie was in the garden uprooting a few favorite plants and distributing them into soil-filled pots. Somehow the orchard's emptiness sounded wrong. Maybe it was that August had always been inhabited by the noise of the workers. Maybe things echoed differently because there was no house to echo off of. Maybe it was just the sound of everyone never coming back.

The sound of a truck coming up the drive drew Birdie's attention. She could just glimpse that it was Leeda. Birdie waved as she climbed out and walked down the path toward her.

"What're you doing?" Leeda asked, putting her hands in her pockets and nodding at the plants.

"We're taking them to Florida. I'm gonna go down with Poopie and my dad before I go back to school." There was a rental house waiting for them there until they could close on a permanent one. It was right by the ocean. Birdie couldn't imagine what waking up to the ocean would feel like.

Leeda stared around the garden. Then her gaze turned to the rows of peach trees across the lawn. "What'll happen to them?"

"They'll get overgrown by other plants, I guess."

Birdie took off her garden gloves and wiped her hand across her brow. Leeda's eyes, like Birdie's, couldn't stop straying to the place where the house had been. It was like they both had to keep reminding themselves it wasn't there.

"Bird, I need to ask you something." Leeda sat down on the bench under the nectarine tree. Birdie sat next to her, warily.

"I've decided not to go back to New York."

"What?"

"My family's gonna flip. Murphy may flip. But it's not right for me."

"What are you gonna do?"

"I'm gonna stay here. I'm gonna go to vet school. Do some online stuff, and then I'll take classes in Atlanta once a week."

Birdie couldn't hide her surprise and confusion. Finally she smiled, scandalized, amazed. "God, what's everyone going to say?" She knew vets didn't make much money. It certainly wasn't what anyone expected for Leeda. Lee was designed to be high profile. She was supposed to be somewhere people could see her and admire her and look up to her.

Leeda plucked a leaf off the nectarine tree and pulled it apart in strings along the veins. "It doesn't matter." Leeda turned to her. "Bird, I want to do something, but it has to be okay with you."

"What?"

"I want to take care of animals. Like a shelter." Leeda tossed her leaf and folded her hands on the back of the bench, turning to face Birdie. "I know that sounds crazy. Like I'm eleven. Like I want to ride unicorns and have a room painted in rainbows and take care of all the homeless animals. But it's really what I want. I want to be helpful in a tiny way."

"I think that's great," Birdie said. She didn't quite understand it, but she trusted Leeda. And Leeda never jumped into anything without weighing it first. In fact, Birdie wasn't sure she'd ever seen Leeda jump, period.

"Bird, I bought the orchard."

Birdie gasped. Leeda plunged on.

"Your dad accepted my offer. But . . ." Leeda got nervous here, plucking another nectarine leaf and tearing it violently. "But I know that it's your place, even if it's not yours anymore. And I don't want to intrude on that. If you don't want me to, if it's too weird or something, I would totally understand—"

Birdie put her hands on Leeda's arm to stop her.

"It's yours," she said. The words came out at the same moment the thought arrived in her brain. She didn't mean, "I'm giving you permission." She didn't mean, "Take it."

Years ago, Poopie Pedraza had stumbled onto the orchard by a twist of fate. Birdie had always thought life would hand it to her next, like that was supposed to be.

But now, saying "It's yours" was only stating a truth.

The orchard had found its way into Leeda's hands while everyone had been looking somewhere else.

It was evening before they had everything packed up, way behind schedule. Leeda had gone home to deal with her parents, a look of utter fear on her face.

Dusk had always been, maybe, the best time at the orchard. It filtered out the distraction of sunlight, throwing into relief the shapes of the dorms, the line of where the air lifted off from the grass, the silhouettes of the peach trees, and the sounds—of a distant dog barking, of the hum of bees.

Birdie walked over to take one last look into the gaping hole where her house had been. She kicked around some of the stones. There was a pile of garbage that had yet to be carted off over by a Dumpster they'd rented. There were old books they'd discarded and boxes Birdie had never even opened. She suddenly felt sad she hadn't explored more. She was out of time.

On impulse, she sifted through the boxes just to get a glimpse. There were old shoes. Some ancient balls of yarn. Two boxes of nails. The only thing that contained anything interesting was a cardboard shoe box. It held a bunch of faded old postcards from Cambodia, Paris, Japan. Birdie skimmed through the pictures like they were little treasures. They promised adventure, beauty, the unknown, the unexpected.

Birdie turned one over and looked at the back. There was no note on any of them. Just the address of the orchard, no person specified, and the postmark. And on the back of each card and drawn in faded blue ink was a tiny heart.

Birdie took one of the postcards to keep. The rest she put back in the box, and she laid it with the rest of the debris.

A few bats already had woken up and were zigzagging this way and that, catching flies. Synchronous fireflies were lighting the shadows between the leaves and the dark spaces nested in blades of grass, hovering right above the ground. Majestic was standing in the truck, paws on the window. The last peaches, the ones that had been missed, were dark spots against the green of the peach leaves—the last color in the spectrum to disappear from sight, the one that stayed the longest, the color of new things.

It was like the end of an animated movie. Like everything that Birdie loved about her childhood home had come out all at once before she left.

Behind her, the truck roared to life as her dad started the engine. Birdie felt the time leaving her; she was aware of only having seconds.

She smiled. In her mind, she said good-bye. She said thank you to whatever or whomever there was to be thankful to.

She ran for the truck and jumped in.

She moved on.

They pulled away.

Thirty-eight

Rex Taggart was packing up his truck in the parking lot of Homewood Suites when Murphy found him.

"You're leaving."

He turned. "Yeah."

"Right before I'm leaving."

"Yeah."

"That's timing."

Rex didn't answer.

Murphy leaned up against the truck and looked at him. "Thanks for beating up my dad, by the way."

"Yeah, usually it's the other way around after you've seen somebody's daughter naked."

Murphy grinned. "Judge Abbott doesn't seem like the fisticuffs kind. I don't think he'd lay a hand on you. Maybe he'd lay a subpoena on you."

Rex laughed under his breath.

"Rex?" Murphy looked at him. "Why did you do it?"

Rex thought. "It didn't seem right, him coming in and shaking up your life when you've come this far without him. It seemed selfish to me. Maybe I was wrong. Your mom kept asking for my advice on everything. I hope you're not too mad at her, Shorts. It was a really hard choice for her. I don't know. Maybe I should have stayed out of it."

Murphy studied her fingers. Rex knew her as well as she knew herself sometimes. But maybe that gave him the same blind spots too. She watched him load the last of his stuff into the truck and shut the door. He turned to her.

"It's good-bye again, huh?" she said, smiling even though it hurt.

"Yeah."

"Rex . . ." She picked at a piece of paint that was chipping off the old truck, and then met his eyes again. "Thanks."

"Yeah. No problem."

He shifted as if he were getting ready to go. Murphy plunged ahead.

"And I wanted to say, I . . . I didn't stop. I didn't stop loving you . . . in that way. That's not why I didn't write. It's the opposite. I mean, I couldn't write because I didn't stop." She was making no sense, but Rex seemed to be calmly getting it.

"I know, Murphy."

"But listen." She bit her lip. "Can we be friends? I want us to be friends. I want us to have each other. Can we, you know, have something long and boring and reliable? Like, maybe I can call you sometimes, when I'm pissed off or when I have something funny to say. Or there's something maybe only you would get?"

He jangled his keys in his pockets and smiled his sideways grin at her. "Murphy, I'm here."

He looked at her as if waiting for something. But finally he gave his keys another jangle, opened the door, and got in his truck.

Murphy backed up, waving to him from her pockets, her thumbs tucked in and four fingers out and waggling.

He nodded at her. Then he turned his attention to the road. As he pulled away, he put a hand out.

Murphy watched him chug down the road, feeling the loss of him.

It hurt enough that she wanted to write him a letter.

Maybe she would.

Thirty-nine

For the first few days of September, Leeda felt like Noah gathering the animals two by two. There was so much building to be done. And she felt like she was pulling each animal out of some kind of flood.

There was a freshly built corral. She'd hired someone to do it. There were the dorms. She was having insulation put into them for winter use, and the men's dorm was being divided into pens. The women's dorm would follow as soon as Leeda could have another place built to live in. But that, like everything else, would take time. Yesterday an article about her had appeared in the local paper. Leeda had been in the local paper many times over the years. But this was the first article that hadn't mentioned traits like "bright," "attractive," "popular," or "straight-A." It had focused on the things she was doing, not on the things she just was. The title, which Murphy had laughed at snarkily over the phone, was LOCAL GIRL MAKES HOOF.

"*Hoof* instead of *good*?" Murphy had asked. "God, typical Bridgewater."

Birdie, who had decided to major in journalism so she could

write about all the things that captured her fancy, found three typos in the online article.

It was a long while before Leeda could find the time to sit down and write a letter. When she finally did, it took her a long time to figure out just what she needed to say.

Dear Mom,

I know you're mad at me right now. I know you think I threw Grandmom's money away. I know you wanted something else for me—something bigger and more important. I think and hope that over time you will change your mind about all these things. I don't think there's anything I can do to show you other-wise, except to let time tell.

I've been thinking a lot about Grandmom, as well as about our family and about our town, or whatever. You're going to laugh, but I've been thinking that maybe Grandmom left the ponies to me because she wanted dirt in the house. I think maybe she wanted life there. I know that it's a stretch, because how could she have known I'd let all the animals in? But I guess I'm saying I believe that, if Grandmom had really had her way—her true way—things would have been allowed to be messy some-times. I like to think maybe she wanted that for me. Messiness.

So I know it's crazy, but sometimes I'm sitting here on the dorm porch, and I think that I'm taking up a place that should have been hers. Like I'm carrying something for her that she couldn't carry. I know that makes no sense. And to be honest, most of all I'm doing it for myself. But sometimes I look around, and I feel like I'm fixing something. Like it's not too late. I feel brave.

I hope you'll come over and visit a lot. Then you can see things from where I sit. I really think I finally know where that is. It feels so good to be home.

I love you.

Love, Leeda

Leeda put the letter in an envelope, addressed it, and sighed.

With Murphy and Birdie gone, Bridgewater seemed a little empty. Leeda had no one to laugh with or to get into trouble with or to go swimming with. Still, she knew she would find people to rely on almost as much as she'd relied on her best friends. It would take time too.

In October, she collected pecans. She watched the fall sunsets from the stairs and called Poopie to ask all sorts of nature questions. By then, her mom had begun to come over for dinner every Wednesday night. Leeda had broken up with Eric the week she had bought the orchard. On Fridays she usually had a date with a guy from vet school.

And then one evening she was sitting on a bench outside the dorm with a week-old kitten and a bottle when a car pulled up the drive.

Leeda had to squint to recognize him at first. He had grown a shaggy beard, and he was wearing a sweater with a hole in it. He looked the picture of everything she would have thought was the opposite of what she'd ever wanted. But her heart jumped into her throat. He walked up to the porch and she stood stiffly. He gave her an awkward hug.

"How was Alaska?" she asked.

"Good. Melting, I guess. How are you?"

"Good." She offered him a spot beside her on the bench, and they sat. She placed the kitten into a box lined with a towel and a heating pad. "I bought this place," she said.

"I know. I read about it online."

Leeda bit her bottom lip, feeling awkward, wondering what to say.

"Are you hiring?" he asked, frowning at her, nervous and true.

Leeda looked at his hand. She debated with herself, and then she reached out and took it.

He squeezed her fingers tightly, and he let out a breath she hadn't noticed he'd been holding. She laid her head on his shoulder, and he kissed the top of her head.

She pulled away. She brought his hand to her face and rubbed it against her cheek.

Some things are easier than you ever thought. That's what it felt like for Leeda to fall in love, for real, for the first time. It felt like it had never been hard at all.

Epilogue

There were so many ways to get between Bridgewater and New York and Florida. There were buses, planes, trains, and cars. Only it can take so much time to get enough money for gas. It was years before Murphy, Leeda, and Birdie were all three together at the orchard again, and by that time, it wasn't anything like it had been.

The year they graduated, Murphy and Rex found they couldn't really be friends and never really had been. They compromised and met in Chicago—where Murphy could have her big-city flair, and Rex could have his outdoors close by, and they could shiver together through the winters in the tiny little apartment they shared. They were married in Bridgewater the following year. Even though she thought it was a sexist tradition, Murphy let her dad give her away. Mr. Taggart had insisted they get married at the Church of the Holy Redeemer. Murphy had insisted they didn't send out invitations. They just put out fliers. Three of the people who showed up had made out with Murphy at some point in time.

Birdie had read a book once called *The Age of Innocence*. Enrico had recommended it. In it, at the end, it was pointed out that one of the main characters had given up the thing she loved most because giving it up meant keeping it beautiful and right. Birdie had tried to look back on this at moments when she felt desperately homesick. But as time went on, she didn't have to remind herself. It became so clear that where the orchard had been, her life had filled itself in with wild colors and soul-shaking experiences and other things as meaningful as peaches and white dirt. Birdie, of all three girls, became the hardest to pin to a specific time and place. She would send Leeda and Murphy and her family cryptic letters with clips of her travel articles from Brazil, from India, from Switzerland, and she would promise to come home soon. But home, it seemed, was something Birdie carried on her back. She finally thought she knew what Poopie had felt when she'd first come to Bridgewater and, seeing shapes in the clouds floating above a place that was completely foreign, found a reason to stay.

Leeda's third year into running the shelter, while Grey was in Atlanta buying supplies, two teenage guys—friends—came walking up the driveway looking for jobs working with the animals. Standing on the porch, they looked like stray puppies. Leeda hired them on the spot. They didn't see the orchard as something that had been lost. They found new spots nearby to swim. They stayed out late. They settled in and grew into the place like trees.

Grey had made a sign and placed it by the door as a joke, but Leeda had kept it. It read *Leeda's Home for Lost Souls*. Below it, Leeda hung a framed photo that Birdie had given her. It was of two Mexican women and three sixteen-year-old American girls: one looking wild and angry; one turning her eyes up, shy and meek; and one standing apart from the other two, thin and perfect, removed and ghostlike.

Without anyone to prune them or care for them, the peach trees slowly died, absorbed by the woods. There was the occasional holdout. A lonely tree here or there that somehow managed to survive and produce ripe, delicious fruit, better than any Leeda could find anywhere. But the last time they were all at the orchard together, Birdie only found one lone blossom, drying up. She took it with her and tucked it in her hair.

What mattered was still there. That was what they all felt, and it was what surprised them all. What mattered couldn't be shaken.

Acknowledgments

My continued gratitude goes to Sara Shandler, as well as Zareen Jaffery, Nora Pelizzari, Kristin Marang, and Elise Howard. Thanks to Glenn Smith at Camp Tall Timbers in High View, West Virginia, for giving me a place to write and spend time with horses. Much appreciation to Barbara Birney of Cause for Paws Animal Shelter in Harper's Ferry, West Virginia, for sharing her time and knowledge. Donations can be made to Cause for Paws at P.O. Box 271, Harper's Ferry, WV, 25425.

Finally, thanks always to my friends and family.

From Darlington Orchard to New York and Mexico City and back again, Jodi Lynn Anderson's national bestselling series tells the tale of a trio of girls who find friendship and more amid the peach trees of Georgia.

jodi lynn anderson

Peaches

National Bestseller

"Peaches *is a sweet and delicious read."*
—Ann Brashares, author of THE SISTERHOOD OF THE TRAVELING PANTS

jodi lynn anderson
National Bestselling Author of Peaches

THE
Secrets
OF
Peaches

"Jodi Lynn Anderson's writing is packed with loveliness."
—Ann Brashares, author of THE SISTERHOOD OF THE TRAVELING PANTS

jodi lynn anderson
National Bestselling Author of Peaches

Love
AND
Peaches

"Jodi Lynn Anderson's writing is packed with loveliness."
—Ann Brashares, author of THE SISTERHOOD OF THE TRAVELING PANTS

From the first peach picked to the last lone blossom, these juicy books will leave you craving more!

An unlikely friendship blooms between Murphy, Leeda, and Birdie, like a peach blossom that even their inevitable separation can't shake from the tree.

Upper East Siders Cate and Andie and British-born Stella and Lola are about to become one big happy family.

Well, *big* anyway.